the detective next door

the detective next door

a novel

w.c. gordon

THE DETECTIVE NEXT DOOR. Copyright ©2020 by W.C. Gordon

For information address:
W.C. Gordon, P.O. Box 984, Jupiter FL 33468

Cover design by Vanessa Mendozzi

ISBN: 978-0-578-68006-4

To my wife... Thank you.

the detective next door

CHAPTER 1

Jesus H. Christ! You have got to be fucking kidding me. Why in the hell was this report taken?

"Perry, listen to this shit! This lady filed a report because somebody talked shit about her on Facebook."

"What?"

"Exactly."

"No, that doesn't make sense. That's not a crime."

"No shit. Apparently, this lady thinks it is. I don't know what's more ridiculous: The fact that this lady had the nerve to file a police report, the fact that one of our officers actually took the police report, or the fact that our sergeant assigned this case for further investigation. Well, the last one doesn't surprise me at all."

"Yeah, that fucking idiot doesn't know his asshole from a hole in the ground."

"You want a coffee?"

"Is there whiskey in it?"

"Bro, it's 9 am?"

"Thank you, 'Big Ben.' Like I said, is there whiskey in it?"

1

And so, I make my second trip to the coffee pot for the day. It's ritualistic at this point. I come in at 7 am, because that is when I am scheduled. The others who are scheduled to come in at 7 am are usually here by 8 am. Not always, but usually. I make a pot of coffee and I go back to my desk. I immediately send out an email. It marks my 'footprint' that I was actually in when I was supposed to be. No thinking required for the email. It was written the prior day and left in the draft folder specifically for this purpose. I sit and drink my coffee, sans whiskey at 7 am, and I surf the internet. Other detectives come in between 8 am and 9 am and finish off the first pot of coffee. The sergeant is scheduled to come in around 9 am and often makes it in by 9:30 am. So, I make the second pot of coffee at 9 am. Sometimes I bring donuts.

Most people tend to talk a lot of shit. Most reasonable people don't talk a lot of shit about the guy that always makes coffee and sometimes brings donuts. They tend to leave that guy alone. I like to be left alone. I am the coffee and donut guy. I do not have a yearning in my heart to provide coffee and donuts for the bureau, but I do have a strong preference to be left alone. I figured out early how to do that and I have exploited it. The boss and the senior detectives like coffee and donuts. I like the resulting treatment.

The 9 am pot of coffee is done. 11 am is the next benchmark: Lunch. Lunch goes til 1 pm. I just have to make it until then when I see it. The red light of doom is illuminated. It stares at me like a wild west gunslinger does at high noon just before the gunfight. Like a bull stares at a matador prior to attack. Like a wife does when you do not load the dishwasher correctly. There is no ignoring it. It will penetrate your brain while every effort is made to avoid eye contact. It haunts your dreams and tortures your soul. My coffee is empty. I know what needs to be done but am formulating every conceivable reason to avoid addressing the task. Finally, like a soldier pinned down in the trenches taking grenades who realizes that his only chance of survival is to charge the enemy directly in a last-ditch effort to overwhelm his foe with speed, momentum, and violence of action, I recognize my fate. This will likely not end well and there will be no medal of honor to be awarded. I eye the light one last time and ultimately press the button. "You have one new message." The voicemail greeting is a British accent. I never understood why. It's annoying but in an annoying way that sometimes supersedes a less annoying voicemail after it so maybe it does serve its purpose. This time it does not. Fuck. It's Facebook Lady wanting me to call her "immediately about the case." She is why I keep Knob Creek in my desk drawer. I hate Mondays.

CHAPTER 2

I just stare at the computer screen. Microsoft Outlook is open and I am getting inundated with emails from Facebook Lady of screenshots from posts and messenger conversations. It is an endless barrage. They just keep coming. Each email, with its screenshot attachment, has a little sentence that reads 'please review and get back to me ASAP!' or 'if this isn't criminal, I don't know what is!' and 'OMG! How is this allowed?!' I stare.

My phone conversation with Facebook Lady went about as well as expected. It turns out that the person talking shit on Facebook is her niece. Well, niece-in-law to be specific. She loved her nephew and heard from him "all the time" and now that he is married, she never sees him. It didn't go over well when I mentioned that I probably see my aunt less since I have been married. That's usually the way things work. Not according to Facebook Lady. While speaking with her, I pulled up their respective Facebook pages on my burner account. Both are public pages and both aunt and niece-in-law seem like a couple of idiots. From what I can tell, the aunt began talking shit to the niece-in-law via private messenger and the niece-in-law began talking shit on the public posts. I have advanced training in narcotics, homicide, and sex crime investigations and now I am relegated to dealing with this.

"She needs to go to jail," Facebook Lady says.

"Not likely ma'am."

"Excuse me? Not likely! And why is it not likely?" Facebook Lady is not quite screaming down the phone yet but I don't think it's far away.

"There is no crime ma'am. This is a civil matter."

Three, two, one...

"ARE YOU FUCKING KIDDING ME?!"

Even with the phone held away from my ear, it was loud.

"You're saying she can slander me like that without repercussions?"

"Libel ma'am." I know I shouldn't say it but I can't help it.

"What?"

"Technically it's libel. Slander is a spoken defamatory comment while libel is written. She wrote on your Facebook page, so..." At least some learning will occur during this conversation.

"I don't fucking care what you call it, it's fucking illegal! That little fucking bitch shouldn't be saying anything about me." Well, maybe no learning will occur after all. And 'little fucking bitch,' huh? I can't imagine why she doesn't like you.

"Are you hearing me, Detective?"

Christ Almighty I wish I wasn't.

"Of course, ma'am. You have my full attention." I say this as I am online buying a new cartridge filter for my pool. I used to get the 100 square foot cartridges but recently changed to the 75 square foot cartridge. I feel like they don't clog up as easily and they are also easier to rinse. I don't notice any difference in the cleanliness of my pool. I usually get the Unicel filters but I found some Pleatco filters for a good price.

"Well?"

Shit, maybe I wasn't hearing everything.

"Ma'am?" As I say this, it occurs to me that not only did I fail to hear what she just said, I also can't remember what her name is. It's written in the case file. Wherever that is.

"How much jail time will she get for this?"

Fuck. My. Life.

"Ma'am, as I mentioned. This is a civil matter. This is not criminal. Being that it is not criminal, there would be no jail time for your niece."

"Niece-in-law!"

"Right, your niece-in-law. As I said, no jail time. You can opt to go after her civilly, but I cannot provide any guidance on that as it is outside of my area of expertise." Area of expertise being actual crimes and not horseshit family drama that my boss should have never burdened me with in the first place. I'm not sure that I have wanted to punch him in the nuts as much as I do now.

"Detective, I have much more evidence to show you regarding the horrible and malicious things that she has done to me."

Horrible and malicious? I have a case right now involving a young woman who was the victim of a home invasion and violent gang rape. To me, that is horrible and malicious. I guess people have different thresholds.

"Would you like me to bring all of this evidence to the police department for us to review together or would you prefer me to email it to you?" She barely was able to finish the sentence when the words "Email will be fine" fell out of my mouth. I realize that the issue needs a little time.

"Ma'am, send me whatever you have. I'll review your documents, reference any recent case law that I may be unfamiliar with, and I will confer with the state attorney about this incident. I will get back to you next week with an update."

"Thank you, Detective. I trust that you will realize the criminal nature after you see all of my evidence." Evidence. Right. I am quite sure I won't be compelled but I just bought myself a week of not having to deal with her on the phone. In the meantime, this can go to the bottom of my pile.

Within seconds of the phone call ending, my inbox begins to fill. The emails seem to be endless and I just stare at the screen in amazement. This lady is consumed. Subject headers such as: 'Illegal. All of this is SOOOOO illegal.' I wonder if she thinks the all caps emphasis on 'so' is going to change my mind about this. As I continue to stare in bewilderment at the seemingly endless stream of emails flooding my inbox, I take notice of a small appendage growing at the entrance to my office. I'd recognize that middle finger anywhere.

"Hey fuckhead, come on in."

Perry steps in, sits down and says, "How did you know it was me?"

"I thought it was your dick at first but then I realized it was way too big for that."

Somewhere buried in his laugh are the words *fuck you*.

Perry leans in over my desk, points to the cubicle next to mine and whispers, "Is she in?"

"Karen?"

Perry gets wide-eyed and panicky while trying to hush me. He whispers, "Yeah."

"No, she took off a little while ago. Said something about an intel meeting down south."

Perry smiles and says, "I'd like to go down south with her. You know what I mean."

I just stare at him.

"You know what I mean?" As he says it, I think he genuinely doesn't think I know what he means.

"Yes, you sick bastard, I know what you mean."

"She's not wearing her ring anymore." He says while raising an eyebrow and giving a coy smile that I do my best to ignore.

"Yeah, I'm aware. Her and her old man are getting a divorce. It's a shame. They have two kids."

"What is a shame is if nobody steps in to help her out if you know what I mean." Same eyebrow and smile. Again, I know what he means.

"Jesus H., Perry. You're not thinking about trying to have sex with her, are you?"

"I'm always thinking about trying to have sex with her. And you should be too. You've seen her tits. They're amazing right?"

"I have not seen them, thank you."

"Don't lie."

"I'm not lying. A buddy dated her in college. Not me."

"Does he have pictures?"

"Bro, that was probably the late 90's. Getting naked pics of a girl isn't like it is today. They would've been Polaroids and they'd probably be all faded out by now anyway. Why am I explaining this? This conversation is over."

"Ok, just one more thing." Again, with the eyebrow and smile. "Are they built for speed or built for comfort?"

"Perry, you have problems bro. Seriously. Anyway, wanna grab lunch?"

"Depends, will Karen and her beautiful breasts be there?"

"Nope, just me and my boobs."

Perry looks at my chest and says, "I'm not impressed."

"I should hope not."

"Ok, lunch it is. In the mood for Giovessi's?"

"That works. You fly and I'll buy." And with that, we go to the favorite cop eating joint in town. It's a great Italian restaurant that has been around since the 1970s. The rumor is that Giovessi ran dope through our town's inlet back in the Cocaine Cowboy days and bridged the gap between the Italians back in New York and the Colombians in Miami. He provided free meals for the chief and his cops back then and never got caught with anything. Nobody knows what level of truth there is to his drug running, but I do know that the free meals that continue for the cops today have helped to keep his son, Sal, who runs the place now, stay out of trouble despite his habit of partying like he is still living in 1980s Miami. I would never personally attest to any cop,

9

specifically me, turning a blind eye to Sal's affinity for the disco dust but I will say that his pepperoni bread is so tasty that it has been known to cause 'situational blindness.'

CHAPTER 3

"So, I just put it against the window and press it?"

"Yeah, that's it. Works better in the bottom corner."

"Why?"

"Fuck, I don't know. Just does. Quiet too. It don't make much noise."

"Really? You don't hear a bunch of breaking glass?"

"You might hear a lil. Not much. Specially if it's tinted. Shit just crumbles. You can pull the whole thing out cause the tint keeps it connected."

"Are you sure about this?"

"You wanna come up or not?! I'm tryin' to get mine. These folks got the shit to spare. Who keeps all that in they car unless they got way more inside? Most prolly don't even know."

"The broken window is a hint, right?"

"Oh yeah, right. Try the handle first. And put your shirt on your hand."

"I got to take my shirt off?"

"No fool, just cover yo damn hand. Ain't tryin' to leave prints."

CHAPTER 4

It's nothing like television or movies. Detective work. It's fulfilling. Sometimes at least. And sometimes I feel like a secretary with a gun. There's no catching the bad guy and getting back out on the road in a thirty-minute episode. I can think of more than one occasion where I spent more time writing a report than the suspect spent in the county jail. All you see on TV is a bad guy getting cuffed and booked and the good guys high fiving each other. No fucking way. There's the rough arrest paperwork. That has all the biographical information of the suspect on it. Don't make a mistake on that. One mistake has the potential to shitcan the entire case. You have to write the probable cause affidavit. Get all the elements of the crime in it or you'll have more problems. The offense incident report. Filing packet request. Witness and evidence list. Photo arrays. Witness statements. CDs or flash drives with electronic data such as videos or pictures. The list goes on and on. Not only do I have to write it all but someone from the State Attorney's Office has to review it. It becomes an exercise in redundancy.

Then there are meetings. Oh my God, how investigators love meetings. They all start the same: "I know every one of you is very busy so I will make this quick so you can get back to your caseload…" Two hours later the meeting comes to an end and you are left thinking, "Why the hell couldn't that have been an email?" The reason is that most people love the sound of their own voice. And their work product, especially if there is a PowerPoint presentation to accompany it. Holy shit! Charts. Graphs. God help you if it is an interactive demonstration that includes some type of layered crime mapping software. "And here you can see all of the aggravated assaults that have occurred in the last thirty days." No one cares. "And if you click this icon, you can see all of the robberies that have occurred during the same timeframe." Still, no one cares. Death. By. PowerPoint! I need a drink.

CHAPTER 5

'On Tuesday, November 8th, 2016 at approximately 0720 hours, officers reported to 16 Hibiscus Dr. in reference to a report of a stolen vehicle. Contact was made with the victim who advised that his blue 2016 BMW 330i was stolen by an unknown suspect(s) sometime overnight. No forced entry was noted and the victim stated that the vehicle was unlocked and the keys were inside.' Every follow up investigative narrative starts the same: A brief synopsis of the incident. This particular synopsis, like many, makes me want to punch the victim.

'During the afternoon hours of 11/8/16, I was assigned this case to further investigate.' That means that this idiot, I mean victim, and his lack of wherewithal to lock his car and not leave the keys inside is now my problem. It's referred to as a 'victim assisted crime' in law enforcement and it's fucking annoying.

It's the usual script with these people.

Victim: "Detective, why was I targeted?"

Me: "You weren't targeted. The suspects were only looking for unlocked vehicles that may have had the keys left inside."

Translation: If you locked your shit, it would still be parked in your driveway.

Victim: "What is the police department doing about this?"

Me: "We have increased patrols in areas that are repeatedly targeted in an effort to deter future crimes." Translation: Apart from holding your fucking hand while you lock your car and remind you on a daily basis to not leave valuable shit in plain sight, we're kind of out of ideas on how to prevent this from happening. You're the reason why my insurance premiums are high.

Victim: "How many agencies have you resourced to recover my car? I love that car. My golf clubs were in the back. I love those clubs."

Me: "Sir, we work very closely with other agencies and utilize a multitude of investigative resources in efforts to locate and recover your vehicle. We have automated license plate readers located throughout the region which will notify me if there is a sighting of your vehicle and the South Florida Task Force, which specializes in stolen vehicles, has been made aware of this particular incident." Translation: Your car is probably in a chop shop in Hialeah or in a shipping container on its way to Dubai. Again, if you locked your shit we wouldn't be having this conversation.

Victim: "I worry that whoever stole my car will come back and target my house. Maybe even me, my wife, or my kids."

Me: "Sir, I can assure you that this was not personal. The suspects were only looking for unsecured vehicles and happened upon yours. They will not be back to target your home."

Translation: These fucking mutts don't even know what neighborhood they were in, sometimes not even the town, let alone be able to find your house in particular. Some kid was pulling on door handles hoping to find one that some dipshit was careless enough to leave unlocked with the keys in it. You're that dipshit, sir.

Me: "Sir, if I may ask: Why were your keys inside of your vehicle?" I already know the answer.

Victim: "Oh, I always leave the keys in the cupholder so I know where they're at and can find them."

Bingo. That's not the first time and sure as hell won't be the last time that I have been told that. It never ceases to amaze me though.

Me: "Sir, have you considered a hook in the garage to hang the keys? Maybe a dish on the stand by the front door?" Translation: Anywhere but inside the fucking car you big dumb dummy!

Victim: "Well Detective, hindsight is 20/20 isn't it?"

Me: "Of course, Sir." I say as I raise an eyebrow that to any reasonable person would be interpreted as a subtle *fuck you*.

As I leave the victim, I let him know that I will be making all efforts to recover his vehicle in a timely fashion and list all the resources that will be utilized. I assure him that I will not rest until I personally find and return his vehicle, letting him know this case is my top priority.

When I get around to returning to the office after grabbing lunch, getting a coffee, picking up a shirt and slacks from TJ Maxx, getting the wife some flowers from Publix and myself a bottle of Knob Creek from the liquor store next to it, I sit down at my desk and type the following: 'Based on my investigation, I have exhausted all possible investigative leads at this time. Due to there being no known suspect(s), witnesses or investigative leads, I will be reclassifying this case from active to inactive until new investigative leads become known. Case status – Inactive.'

Done and on to the next waste of time.

CHAPTER 6

"You been in this neighborhood before?"

"No, I don't think so," Nathan said as convincingly as he could. Truth is he had been in this neighborhood many times before. He lived in the neighboring town as a kid. When he was in his early teens, he played soccer with the local athletic association. This was before his father died. His father, a well-known physical therapist, sponsored the soccer team. Nathan never really noticed how white the neighborhood, or his soccer team, was. He was acutely aware of it now.

"These white folks always leave they cars open. We gonna find one with a key tonight. I feel it."

"What do we do if we find a key?"

"What the fuck you think? We take it. Whip it all night before it's reported. Dump that shit in the morning. Maybe sell it for a hundo."

"Oh."

"What you mean oh?!"

"I found a key last time. I didn't think of that. I only took the earbuds."

"You a muthafuckin fool. Earbuds. Fuck. Coulda had the car but you take the fucking earbuds. You remember the car? We can go back and take it? They probably even got new earbuds fo yo ass!"

"No, I don't remember," Nathan said. In fact, he did remember. He remembered thinking that was an easy way for someone to get their car stolen. The thought of stealing the car never crossed his mind. Nor did taking the pistol that he saw in the glove compartment. He knew he needed something for his efforts and grabbed the earbuds in the center console.

"Hey Kevin, you sure you want to do this again tonight?"

"It's *Kodak* fool."

"Yeah, sorry. Kodak. Are you sure it's worth going out tonight?"

"Every night son. I'm trying to get licks. We trying to come up. My homeboy gonna drop us off. We getting a car tonight, I fucking feel it."

"Ok." Nathan was sure he hadn't convinced his cousin. He hadn't nearly convinced himself. 'Go through the motions' he thought. His goal was not that of getting a car, like Kodak. He just did not want to get caught. He was leaving for the Miami MEPS in a few weeks. All he wanted to do was make his mother proud. If he could do that and not disappoint his cousin in the meantime, he would accomplish both.

CHAPTER 7

"President Trump. President Donald J. Trump. You have got to be fucking kidding me." I'm staring at the computer screen.

"Would you prefer the alternative?" Perry looks at me with a genuinely inquisitive look.

"Absolutely fucking not!" I snap back still staring at the screen.

"At least this one likes cops."

"Look, I'm happy that he is an open supporter of the military and law enforcement. That's a nice change compared with what we have been dealing with for the past eight years but really, Donald Fucking Trump?"

"That's President Donald Fucking Trump to you!"

"When The Simpsons become prophetic about presidents, you know we have a problem."

"Hey, The Simpsons are an American treasure. And who can resist Marge? Hashtag, super sexy milf!"

I just look at Perry.

He smiles and says, "Don't act like you're not into the blue-haired women."

"You have a problem bro. And please don't ever use the word 'hashtag' around me again. I'm a grown man. But seriously, what kind of precedent does this set? It's a popularity contest now."

"Isn't it always?" Perry looks slightly confused.

"It's always a popularity contest between politicians or political parties. Celebrities have stayed out of the presidential arena."

"What about Reagan?"

"He was the governor of California before he was the pres. And don't bring up Arnold or Jesse the Body because they didn't run for president. Now we have a legit reality TV star in the White House. We didn't get the president we wanted but we got the president we deserve. You wait. It will be President Kardashian or President The Rock soon."

"Hell yeah, The Rock is the fucking man and Kim K is hot!"

I just stare at Perry. From the look on his face, he can tell by the look on my face that I am not amused.

"Well, at least it's not Hillary."

With that, I have to agree.

CHAPTER 8

"How about that election?" He just awkwardly stands there. The ability to project your authority to others in your environment is called command presence. My supervisor has none. It would be easy to ignore him except due to his obesity, he is blocking the entrance to my office.

"Good morning, Sarge. What's up?"

He continues to awkwardly stand in the threshold. I find it telling of his leadership style. Not willing to make a decision. Not in the office but not out of it either. What a terrible way to live your life. I know he wants something. I want to shout at him 'Just fucking say it!' but I don't. I just stare. He doesn't stare back. He just kind of looks around me. He looks at a picture on the wall. It is a picture of me taken at one of Saddam's palaces. He looks at me looking at him and looks away again. For Christ's sake man, grow a pair.

"How's your caseload right now?"

Questions like this irritate me even more than his awkward presence. You are my supervisor. You know how my caseload is or at least you should. It's fucking huge. Please don't ask me dumb questions. And please, for the love of God, don't ask me for an update on the Facebook Lady case.

"Whatcha got, Sarge?"

"I just got a call from the road sergeant. They're out with a dead guy. Looks drug-related. They're going to want a detective out there." As he says it, he's staring at his feet. RoboDoc would have a field day with this guy!

"Who found him?" For me, that is an important question for all death investigations. Not for the investigative aspect of it, mind you, I just hope that it is a family member who found the decedent. That saves me from having to do a death notification. Besides cases involving kids, doing a death notification is the hardest part of the job for me. Having to break the news to a parent, spouse, loved one, whoever, is awful. Watching their world crumble in front of you totally sucks.

"The mom found him."

Thank you, Jesus.

"I'll handle it boss."

"Are you sure? I can get someone else to go out there."

Really? Can you? Then why the hell are you here bothering me with it? Oh, that's right, you knew I wouldn't piss and moan about handling it.

"Don't worry Sarge, I'll take care of it. I'll give you a shout if there are any signs of foul play." Not because he will be any help of course. Only because he will send Big D and Karen out there to bask in the glory of a big case. Either way suits me fine. Plus, I like OD cases. They're easy and stay in your active cases while you wait for the medical examiner to send toxicology reports. It makes me look busier than I actually am.

"Thanks. I appreciate it. I'll get you back."

No, you won't.

"Is that you in that picture?"

"Yep. That was back when I was a heartbreaker and lifetaker. Now that I am married, there's no more heartbreaking." I just stare at him. And with that, he gets the idea and vacates my office.

As I arrive at the crime scene, I am happy to see an old Ford Crown Victoria police car parked out front. The agency downed all of our Vic's about six years ago. All except one. Bobby's Vic. Bobby is the saltiest cop that I know. This guy has been a cop in this town since it still had its old small-town charm. This guy has some great stories. Most of the cops who grew up here have some story about 'Bobby the Cop' from when they were kids. He's never been anything but a road cop. He's never wanted to be. He's a cop's cop and just a damn good guy. Everyone likes Bobby. He has no rank but has a huge amount of influence. He has been a cop almost as long as our Chief of Police has been alive. Because of that, he's granted the courtesy of having whatever police car he damn well pleases. And he wants his Vic.

"Hey Bobby. How are you, Sir? Still keeping the Vic running I see."

"Hey there, young man. Good to see you." At nearly forty, it feels slightly odd being called 'young man' but I can't complain. "Ole 'Vicky.' Yep, she will run forever. That's the last real cruiser made. These new things are garbage." Bobby glances at another officer's Chevy Impala and gives it a cold look.

25

"The new Chargers aren't bad."

"Aren't bad?! You're a hell of a salesman." Now Bobby is giving me a cold look. "Aren't bad also means aren't good. Take a curb at 50 in one of those things and the ass end will fall off. Vicky will eat that curb up. That being said, I never should have gotten rid of my Dodge Diplomat. Best cruiser I ever had."

I just smile. I can listen to this guy for hours.

"360 V8. Amazing car! I used to pray for people to run from me in that car. Of course, that was back in the good old days when you could still chase anyone who ran."

You gotta love this guy.

"Did I ever tell you about the fella who robbed the old town bank?"

I've heard this story many times but it never gets old.

"We get a call that the bank was robbed at gunpoint so there I go, speeding to it in my old Diplomat. I get on scene and they tell me the fella ran off towards the train station." I do love listening to this guy. This town has to have two dozen banks now and he tells of a time when there was only one. And the train station shut down sometime in the early 1980s. "So, they gave me the description and I go looking for this guy. Anyway, enough time goes by and I think I see someone who matches what they said. And sure enough, as soon as he sees me, he goes a'running! I drove as far as I could and had to get out running myself. I stopped the Diplomat at the tire shop and ran past the fishing store that was on the canal there. I cut too tight around the corner and there he was, gun a'pointin at me! Sonofabitch fired a shot at near point-blank range. I don't know how, cause I was running full speed, but I still managed to fall backward right on my ass. I think I thought I was shot. I think he also thought I was shot. He turned around and ran off and once I realized that I wasn't dead, you know what I did?" I sure do but I am not going to say. This is my favorite part. "I broke leather and shot that sumbitch. Well, I shot at him I should say. I unloaded every bullet in that old revolver and you know what happened?" I do. I say nothing and just smile. "He just kept a'running. I missed him with every shot. But you know what I heard?" Yes, I do. "I heard a woman scream at the top of her lungs. I thought, 'Aw, shit. I missed him but I just killed a lady.' I spent the rest of the shift expecting someone to call and say that their dear old grandmother had been shot dead. Took the Chief an hour to calm me down and assure me that I hadn't killed anyone. Back in those days, I wouldn't have gone to prison or anything. Probably would've got a day or two off work though if I had. Anyway, the Chief let me leave an hour early so I could blow off some steam before going home. And wouldya guess where I went?" I sure can. "I went to Ralph's Bar. And would you guess who was there?" Yep, sure can. "That sumbitch who shot me. Or shot at me. Well, I jumped on him like a rabid dog and beat him six ways from Sunday. Called the Chief from the bar and that sumbitch went to jail. I didn't pay for beers at Ralph's for a week after that! Best week ever." That story never gets old.

"You going to try and relive that shooting experience later today on the range?" I ask.

"I'll never qualify if I shoot like that! You going today?"

"If I can make quick work of this, I'll head out there to shoot the qual course. So, Bobby, what do you think happened here?"

"Looks like a cut and dry overdose. Mom says he's struggled with dope for years. Says he's done heroin in the past. He probably got a hot shot this time. Probably cut with that new shit. What's it called?"

"Fentanyl."

"Yep, that's the stuff. You're the expert with it so you'll know better than me."

With that, I have to laugh. A cop like Bobby has forgotten more about dope, and street-level police work in general than I know. Probably more than I will ever know.

"Anyway, she's next door with the neighbor so you got the place to yourself. Make all the noise you want, he won't mind." And with that Bobby laughed. 'He' of course is the decedent. Cops have totally fucked up senses of humor. You need to in this job; otherwise, it will eat away at you. My wife calls it a 'coping mechanism.' Not necessarily a healthy one, but one nonetheless. As I enter the home, I look back at Bobby. He's about to light up a cigarette. Marlboro Reds. Cowboy Killers. Our agency has a strict no tobacco policy. Again, no rank but plenty of influence. I love that guy.

As I enter the residence, I take quick stock for my report. No signs of a struggle. Tidy but not too clean. Items where they should be but not perfectly placed. Don't be complacent. Treat every death investigation like it is a homicide and you won't get caught with your pants down when it is one. Check the entire house and go into where the recently expired is last. Go back out the same way. Sometimes you may notice something that wasn't there the first time after seeing the departed.

There he is in all his deceased glory: Slumped over on the floor in a quasi-praying pose. Face mashed directly into the floor. The usual discharge from the nose and mouth. The usual set of user ink. Tattoos like praying hands, 'No Regrets' and 'Only God Can Judge Me.' No dipshit, I will judge you as well. You're 23 and living in your mom's house snorting caps. I will judge you. You're an asshole. Mattress on the floor. No frame or headboard. Probably sold for dope. Old PlayStation but no TV. Sold for dope. Jitterbug cell phone. Can't get a proper phone carrier. Fighting Irish poster haphazardly taped to the wall. You probably can't name the town Notre Dame is in. I have no patience for this. I grew up with this.

Okie dokie, let's find what I'm looking for. Garbage can, nothing. Around the body, nothing. Drawer of the nightstand... Bingo. Clear cap with an off-white powdery residue. Perfect, there's my OD. Anything else... There it is. So predictable. Nothing says hiding spot like an air conditioning vent with only one out of the four screws holding it to the ceiling. Step up on the bed and move the vent. Medicine bottle. Inside, a small baggie and one capsule filled with powder. Boom, done.

Quick call to the medical examiner. Tell her it's showing all the signs of a 'narcotic related accidental overdose' and the phone call ends. They've declined to come out and are going to send the body snatchers. Sorry, the removal service for the recently deceased. My job is done. And in six to twelve weeks, I'll get the toxicology report from the ME and close the case.

Now to go give the mom my deepest sympathy. I assure her that the police department will do their utmost to bring to justice the murderers that sold her son that "terrible drug." Blah, blah, blah. "Yes ma'am, we work closely with the DEA. Yes, ma'am, we will exhaust every resource until the dealer is located and arrested for murder." I hate to make false promises but it is easier for them to handle. Telling the truth that their son or daughter or husband or whatever, willingly purchased, consumed, and subsequently overdosed on drugs is their own fault does not go over well. I know. I've heard that line. It was not well received.

Now for the hardest part: Figuring out where to go for lunch.

CHAPTER 9

Friday. One hour in. Seven to go. So far, so... Fuck.

"Hey, what have you got going on today?"

That is a loaded question. The boss asking that question is never good and there is virtually no successful way to answer it.

"I'm buried under paperwork, Sarge. Totally swamped."

"Great! Take the new guy. Show him some of the magic you work back here. It's his bureau day."

Every newly hired cop has to go through a field training program once they get hired. There are various phases of the training and at certain points, they get put with specialty units to see what they do and get a little insight of the totality of the job. Spend a day with the dog cops and learn about canine police work. Go out on the boat with the marine unit for a day. And of course, spend a day with a detective. Taking one of the new guys is usually awful. It's not that I don't like to bequeath my knowledge upon a young officer who may have aspirations to be an investigator one day. It's that most of these new cops have watched too much TV growing up and they think the job is super-awesome and all about solving the crime and locking the bad guy away in prison all in a thirty-minute episode. I have to be the bad guy that lets them know that a detective is basically a secretary with a gun and there is a huge amount of paperwork that goes into each investigation, many of which end up with the state not wanting to pursue prosecution. You'd be amazed how many cases get a 'no file' status by the State Attorney's Office. Many criminals walk free because unless you gift wrap the case for the state, they don't usually make the effort. The squeaky wheel gets the grease and a few times an 'anonymous' call may have been made to a local news station about cases the state shit-canned. It's amazing how quickly the state will reopen a case if they hear that the public might catch wind of their ineptitude. Luckily, I have a 'friend' who is willing to make that call to the station.

The new cops come in here all wide-eyed and wanting to save the world. They want to learn the mystique of the gold badge. I don't like being the one to break it to them. That and I heard the new guy is a weirdo.

"Sarge, come on. I got a lot of shit to get done. I don't want to bore the new guy." That's code for I really don't want to have to explain every little detail of what I do to this guy who hasn't even done a traffic stop yet. "Plus sarge, I'll be honest. I heard the new guy is a fucking weirdo." As the word "weirdo" rolled off of my tongue the new guy, who was standing outside of my door the entire time, turned the corner and walked into my view.

I look at the new guy who is looking at me and then I look at Sarge who was also looking at me. I look back at the new guy and say, "Have a seat new guy. I'm gonna go grab a coffee. Want one?"

"Whatever you do, I'll do, Detective!"

Fuck, this is going to be terrible.

Sergeant has a shitty smirk on his face, turns, and goes waddling down the hallway toward his office.

I head over to the coffee pot and grab two cups from the cabinet.

Perry looks at me and says, "Two cups?"

"Don't ask."

"Hell yes, you got the new fuck today!" and he starts to laugh.

Without looking at Perry I slowly extend my left fist toward him and methodically lengthen my middle finger as I pour two cups with my right hand.

I return to my office and put one of the cups in front of the new guy.

"What flavor is this?"

This is going to be a long day.

"The flavor is 'lukewarm black.' Enjoy."

As the new guy is trying to drink his coffee without having to hold his nose, the boss walks back into my office.

"It's your lucky day," he says to nobody in particular.

Nothing good will come of this.

"Dead guy in a car at the dealership on Windsor Road. Go check it out."

Three, two, one...

"Hell yeah, that's awesome!"

Ahhh, the allure of being a new police officer and everything being a 'who done it' caper.

"It's not awesome," I say.

"Sorry, I didn't mean it like that. I just figured that it gives us a chance to work a case together. A dead guy in a car sounds like a serious crime. Maybe it's a mafia hit or a gangland murder!"

I just stare at him. He has so much to learn and I really should not shatter his hopes and dreams just yet; however, he does need to be brought down to reality a little bit.

"Ok, let's get a few things straight. For a start, we're not Riggs and Murtaugh."

The new guy just stared at me. From the blank expression on his face, our age gap became immediately obvious.

"You've never seen Lethal Weapon, have you?"

"No. Sorry sir."

This is going to be a long day. I feel old.

"Anyway, don't make out like this is some type of major murder. It's a dead guy in a car. People die in cars all the time. Probably an OD or a suicide. Definitely not a murder."

"Why wouldn't it be a murder, Sir?"

"Well, for it to be a mafia hit we would need to have a mafia presence in this town. And for it to be a gang-related murder we would needs gangs in this town."

"Sir, I heard that we have gangs."

"We have wannabes. Big difference. Anyway, if it was a murder, we would not be going to it. Murder cases are the sexy cases and those cases go to Big D and Karen." Shit, I slipped. 'Big

D' is the nickname for Dara Hill, the most senior detective in the bureau.

"Who's 'Big D?'"

"Like I said, the big cases go to Karen and Dara."

"So, you're not the sexy detective?" says the new guy.

"Don't get me wrong, I'm sexy as fuck!" The new guy doesn't laugh at my joke. My wife calls that a 'dad joke.'

"Anyway, big cases like homicides get handled by more senior detectives who have more experience." What that really means is that there are a few detectives who want the spotlight of working the high-profile cases. I have all the qualifications to work homicides but none of the interest. Homicides are a pain in the ass and usually garner huge media attention in this town. Dara and Karen love the attention. I don't want any of it. I'll take all the bullshit cases and they can deal with that nonsense.

"It could be a murder though, right?"

I just look at the new guy, "Sure, it could be a murder."

When we get to the dealership on Windsor, I park and we walk under the yellow crime scene tape. With that act, the new guy just about loses his cool. I remind him that the officer maintaining the crime scene log has more time backing his patrol car up to a curb than he does as a cop. Gotta keep his feet on the ground.

I make contact with the primary officer and get the basics. "Fifty-three-year-old white male. Cleaning lady found him. He's the overnight security guy. Sitting in the front seat of his minivan. Last seen alive around 11 pm when the sales manager left."

"The sales manager was here til 11?"

"Yeah, he told me he was here doing paperwork. I called BS and he ultimately fessed up to the truth." The officer advised.

"Let me guess, he was banging his side chick here late night."

"You are a great detective! His side chick is the receptionist here. He doesn't want you to put that in the report though."

"Tell him not to worry, I'll say he was here doing paperwork." I use air quotes while saying 'paperwork.'

I walk the new guy over to the decedent. The recently expired is sitting in the driver's seat of an old shit box Dodge Caravan. He is slumped backward between the driver's seat and passenger's seat, staring at the headliner of the vehicle. Lividity and rigor are consistent with body positioning and the deceased has released his bowels. He looks to be near 300 pounds and about 5'10". There is an iPad sitting on the dashboard and his cell phone is in plain view in the center console area. He's wearing a worn-out old gun belt and what looks to be a very worn and rusted Beretta 92FS is in the holster. The zipper of the dead one is down and I think I see something resembling the 'tip of the spear' in the opening of his fly. I look over at the new guy.

"You going to puke new guy?"

He manages to whisper something that vaguely sounds like "No."

"You've never seen a dead person before, have you?"

The new guy just looks at me and nods his head. This is where I have to put everything into perspective. Most people don't see anyone who had shed their mortal coil unless it is a family member at a funeral. Being able to stand over a dead body and talk about last night's football game is something only a few types of people can do. Detectives are one of those types of people.

"Why don't you go to the bathroom and freshen up. We will talk about this guy when you return."

With that said, the new guy turns and runs to the bathroom. A good puke will help him.

While he's gone, I have a closer look around the scene. Nothing suspicious or criminal in nature found. I was kind of hoping there would be something. Without that, I am left to build on my hunch. I really don't want to view what was last seen on that iPad. The new guy is back.

"So new guy, what do you think happened here?"

"Sir, my name is Travis." I just stare at him. "Uh, maybe this guy was poisoned." I continue to stare at him. "A jealous coworker or ex-lover maybe?" I stare. "Did you find a note, sir? Maybe it was a suicide." My intent stare changes to just a concerned look. Not concerned for his safety or well-being. Concerned for the future of law enforcement.

"Porn," I say.

"Sir?"

"What kind of porn do you think we will find in the search history of that iPad?"

"Sir?"

"Items of value in plain sight and reach. The gun. Cell phone. iPad. Nothing is taken, so it's likely not a robbery. The dude is morbidly obese and his zipper is down. That iPad is strategically placed."

Now the new guy is staring at me.

"The dude's wall is down and his Pink Floyd is coming out."

The new guy does not get this reference either. I still feel old.

"Open up the iPad and see what his search history shows. I call BangBros."

The new guy looks at me and says, "Don't we need a search warrant or something like that?"

"Nope." I stare and realized that this can be a teaching moment. "Dead people don't have a reasonable expectation of privacy and we do not need a search warrant. We're conducting an investigation." I look at him. I want to tell him not to ever question me again.

"Open his iPad."

I was wrong. It wasn't BangBros. It was YouPorn but the concept was the same.

"So, new guy. What we have here is a fat dude, trying to pass the time by jacking off. He probably had a heart attack. So, I'll call the medical examiner and they will send the body snatchers to take this dude to the morgue for an autopsy. Welcome to the illustrious world of detective work."

As I say this, an officer comes up to me and lets me know that the surveillance video from the dealership is ready to view. On 'Camera 4' the minivan can be seen. The officer says that nobody else is seen in the video. I look over at the new guy and ask if he wants to see someone masturbate themself to death. He turns white and promptly makes his way to the bathroom again.

CHAPTER 10

Thank goodness the new kid had his fill of detective work after that call. I brought him back to the office, showed him a few things but he couldn't seem to get his color back. I seized the opportunity to be the 'cool detective.'

"Hey new guy, you've seen plenty today. Why don't you pack it in early and head home?"

"Sir, I don't mind staying."

"It was a rhetorical question. Call it a full day on your time card. Go home, make yourself a drink, put your feet up and relax."

"But I don't drink, Sir."

I just stare at him. He got the idea.

"Don't worry about leaving early. I'll cover for you. I have hours of typing boring reports and that is no fun for you to watch. It will be a late one for me."

He stands up, shakes my hand, and does a light jog out of the bureau. Perfect. Two birds. He thinks I'm some awesome guy for shouldering the workload and letting him go early and I got rid of him. Not to do any work, mind you. I gave him about a two-minute head start to get out of the building. Then I logged off my computer and made tracks for the day. Anything past noon on a Friday in the bureau is unheard of unless there's some major caper being worked. That and the boss has been gone for at least an hour. I would hate to stay and make him look bad. Although he always references a 'meeting' at another department that he has to attend. In all my years, I've never heard of a meeting on a Friday afternoon. We all know the score. Whatever... Everyone has their hustle.

I run home and get a few chores done before the wife gets home from work. I always beat her home on a Friday by a few hours. She leads counseling groups on Friday afternoons and is usually one of the last ones out of her clinic. No biggie. She loves it. She has Mondays off, so she has her time too.

The weather is perfect. Sun is shining brightly. It's gonna be a warm fall weekend in South Florida. Now for the big Friday evening decision. Is it going to be a booze cruise on the boat, a ride on the Harley or a drive in the old CJ. I am the envy of all my friends. Well, all of my friends with kids. They are dealing with their dirty little booger eating children all weekend long and I am busy deciding where to drink. A buddy of mine calls my relationship a DINK; dual income, no kids. No complaints for me. Truth is, I never really wanted kids. The military just solidified that. Something about radiation exposure while in Iraq. I'm shooting blanks now. Kids aren't even an option. I don't advertise that or anything. It just is what it is. And the wife? She doesn't mind one bit.

I decide on a little booze cruising in the boat. It was my first purchase when I got back from the military. I didn't even have a vehicle yet and had to borrow a buddy's truck to get it home. I love this little boat. Being on the water always means it feels a little cooler than usual so I am sure to throw a few sweatshirts inside of the front hatch along with a blanket. I pack the Yeti with ice, two bottles of champagne, a twelve-pack of PBR, and a small bottle of Jack Honey. It is a little much for two people but I prefer to be prepared. I would hate to be stranded and not have enough booze.

Within a few hours, and a few beers, Nic pulls into the driveway. I can see the smile on her face through the windshield when she sees the boat hooked up to the back of the truck. She parks and without stopping to kiss me runs into the house. Within five minutes she is out, wearing a canary yellow sundress with my favorite bikini of hers underneath and she is jumping into the passenger seat. She pounces on me across the bench seat of the old F150. I am the happy recipient of a wet and loving kiss.

"I was hoping we would get the boat out!" she says with a smile.

"I figured a booze cruise was in order. With the family stuff we've had going on the last few weekends, I wanted to give the old girl a run. The boat I mean, not you." I give her a little grin. She rolls her eyes in the way I am more than used to and says, "Enough with the dad jokes, get us to the water!"

"We live in paradise. People vacation where we live. You believe that?" she says with an intoxicating smile.

41

I can't take my eyes off of her. She looks stunning. My everything.

"Seriously babe, I love where we live." Her body is silhouetted by the setting sun outlining every curve through a nearly translucent dress.

I reach into the cooler and pull out a bottle of Veuve Clicquot and give Nic a little smile. "Will you do the honors?" I say. She loves to pop a bottle of champagne and I love to watch. She lets out the same giggle every time she does it which solicits the same laugh from me each time. By the time the second bottle gets popped, our synchronized laughing turns into an all-out giggle fit. She always makes me laugh. I swear I didn't laugh for years before meeting her.

Halfway through the second bottle, the sunset is to our distant left and the lighthouse to our right. The yellow sundress dress draped over the center console. Bikini bottoms somewhere. My flip flops being used as padding between the deck of the boat and knees of the beautiful woman bent in front of me. The tranquil waters are now lapping against the side of the hull.

CHAPTER 11

Saturday morning begins the way most of them do. Sleeping in. Snuggling. Lovemaking. Breakfast making (by me). Walking the dog. Usually in that order but not always.

"I think we should see Pop today," Nicole says. Her eyes welling slightly.

I look up as I plate her omelet and see that she has a concerned look.

"Nan texted me. He didn't have a good night."

It's so sad to watch. She loves her grandparents. What's not to love? They are genuinely great people. Sweet. Kind. Generous. I never really knew my grandparents. Our upbringings were quite different but I completely understand her emotions. Nobody wants their loved ones to die and you sure as hell don't want to watch it. But you can't not watch it. You have to look no matter how bad it hurts because it will hurt you more, and for much longer, if you don't look.

"You don't have to come. I know it's not how you want to spend your Saturday."

I look at her. She kinda looks ridiculous. She's sitting there wearing one of my shirts, three sizes too big for her, has her hair in this messy 'top but falling to one side bun' kind of thing, and she did a seriously half-ass job of removing her makeup last night before bed. Despite that, and looking like she may cry at any second, she is the most beautiful thing I have ever seen.

"Nic, I'll come to the hospital with you. That is how I want to spend my Saturday. With you." I walk over and pull her into me for a hug. She wraps her arms around my waist and sobs gently. Between sobs, she says that we can take the bike to the hospital so we can still get some motorcycle time today. I do love my wife.

CHAPTER 12

Fear. That's the most accurate description of the look I see on his face. Not only fear. There is also frustration, desperation, and confusion. Primarily just fear though. I suppose that's an understandable reaction to have when you're face to face with a naked man pointing a gun at you. I know how this will end.

If you're not familiar with a Safariland level three retention holster, then it's fairly difficult to remove the gun from such a holster. That's the point. It helps to protect the wearer of said holster from having their gun taken from them as you can't just pull the gun out. You need to apply pressure, rotate a 'hood' forward from atop the weapon, and push a locking mechanism forward with your thumb. In that order. If you don't know that, you may end up standing in front of a nude man who has a gun pointed at you while trying desperately to draw the gun that you have in that holster.

All department policies require that you remove any firearms from your vehicle when you are not in them to prevent the weapon from being stolen during a vehicle burglary. Guns get left in vehicles. A lot. Apparently, I left mine in my vehicle last night.

My home surveillance system can be viewed from an app on my phone. A feature of that app is a notification option when motion is detected; you are notified via an alert on your phone. I was woken up by that notification. I keep a loaded Springfield XD-9 subcompact 9mm handgun in my nightstand. I also sleep naked.

When my wife and I were looking to buy our first home, we had an idea of what we wanted: three bedrooms, a garage, a big backyard, close to the town center. Like most, we also had a budget. We were able to find a home that was exactly what we were looking for; however, there were concessions that had to be made. It was very near the railroad tracks.

Living near a railroad has a few obvious pitfalls, such as the high levels of train noise at various times throughout the day and night. That, combined with my snoring, causes my wife to wear earplugs when she sleeps. There are not many benefits to those facts except when you need camouflage noise to conceal the sound of a gunshot.

Naked. Expect for the gun I am holding; I am wearing only my birthday suit. The gun is trained on the chest, center mast, of the subject standing in front of me. My eyes are trained on his, looking for any fight or flight indicators. He has the grip of my department issued Glock 22 .40cal handgun in his right hand. He is holding the holster, still attached to the remainder of the duty belt, with his left hand. I rarely use that duty belt now that I am in plain clothes for my day to day work. It was in there for firing range training that we had. Two days ago. I was lucky having left it in the car for one night untouched. Unfortunately, not for two.

Hooded sweatshirt and gloves. The subject is wearing a hooded sweatshirt and gloves. In South Florida. I am completely nude and sweating. Not because I am nervous but because even in the midnight hours, the humidity is still high along with the temperature. He has the complete burglar uniform on: hooded sweatshirt, sweatpants, gloves, and, of course, slides. I can never understand why anyone wears slides when committing crimes. You're not going to run away from anyone with your urban Jerusalem cruisers on. Strangely enough, he seems to be alone. Alone means local and I've never seen him before.

As the clouds part ways in the night sky, the moon illuminates the young man opposite me. I see his hands still fumbling in their attempts to free the gun from the holster and level the playing field. I see the Trijicon front sight post of my pistol glowing against the backdrop of his chest. I hear what I immediately recognize as the hood of the holster being thrown forward and the click of the locking mechanism disengaging. The moonlight hits his eyes perfectly as I watch both pupils constrict. The constriction may be a result of luck or fear. His luck in freeing the firearm or his fear in the near-deafening sound of an approaching train's horn. The sound that up until this very moment I have despised but now provides me with the warm blanket of protection that I have been waiting for.

CHAPTER 13

Mike is a good neighbor. He is the kind of neighbor that I have always wanted. The kind that leaves me alone. That preferred behavior is obviously reciprocated by me. I respect his privacy and he respects mine. The most obtrusive action my side of the fence has ever taken is when my wife brings him baked goods about once a year. The most obtrusive thing he does is bring my garbage cans up from the side of the road after the trash man comes. My kind of neighbor.

We talked when I first moved into the house. He is a veteran but didn't talk about his service and I didn't talk about mine. Just a mutual respect for each other and our privacy. Guessing by his age, I'd put him as a Vietnam vet. And judging by the fleet of old cars in his backyard, I'd put him as a frustrated mechanic. As far as I am concerned, he can have an entire junkyard behind his house as long as he leaves me alone.

"Babe?"

"Yes, Nic?"

"Can you come to the door?"

I have spent most of my morning contemplating how to handle my current situation. Not an easy task by itself, coupled with acting normal so as to not alarm the wife is increasingly difficult. Now to make matters worse, my perfect up until a few minutes ago neighbor Mike is at my front door.

"What do you mean he's at the door?"

"I mean Mike, our neighbor, is at the front door of our house. What is so difficult to understand about that concept? Invite him in for coffee. He's always so nice." I do love that she is so welcoming and kind. It's a nice counterbalance in our relationship. However, her current level of hospitality is ill-timed.

"Tell him I'm busy."

"Busy? It's Sunday morning. How busy are you supposed to be? If you don't go out there and talk to him, then he will be sitting at the breakfast table with us and you'll be forced to talk to him."

There are times in your life when an impression that you have of somebody is entirely confirmed. This is one of those times.

I open the door, step to the patio, and shut the door behind me. I realize that this is the closest that Mike has ever been to my home. "Good morning Mike, how are ya?"

"Walk with me."

Mike does not give me the option to contest or query as he immediately about faces and walks down my driveway to the area between our homes. It takes a bit of effort to keep up with him and I study his gait. Strong, authoritative and with a deep purpose. Three attributes that I am lacking at this moment.

Mike turns and I stop a few paces away from him. He quickly makes up the distance and with the lack of personal space afforded by most drill instructors he says, "What is your plan?"

"Pardon me?"

He looks wholeheartedly unimpressed and checks all surrounding sectors of fire before commencing a full assault of knowledge upon my position.

"It's going to be near 90 degrees today and humid. That body will decompose quickly under that tarp. You basically made an oven for it."

What. The. Fuck.

His assault of knowledge was so swift, silent, and deadly that not only was I unable to man my battle stations, but I was unable to get out of my bunk in time for the attack. I cannot quite imagine what the look on my face held, but judging by his facial expression it was one of extreme bewilderment.

"While a train will conceal a gunshot to most, I have heard enough in my time to distinguish it among any other sounds regardless of how loud."

I just continue to stare. I have never been so confounded in my entire existence.

"The gunshot I can live with. I can even stomach seeing you in your birthday suit dragging a dead Afro-American fella to the side of your house. But I'll be goddamned if I'm going to be subjected to smelling that for the rest of the day. And I sure as hell am not going to let a crime scene happen within feet of my property. No fucking news crews around here, thank you very much."

The walk back to the front door felt like a year had elapsed since I crossed that threshold.

"Nic?"

"What did Mike want? He looked serious."

"He is having trouble with one of his cars and needs an extra set of hands. I told him I'd help him but it's probably going to take a while. Why don't you give your sister a call and see if she wants to meet you out for brunch? You can take the Jeep and make a day of it."

"Aw, I was hoping to spend the day with you. 'Sunday Funday' like we always do. Maybe I'll have Sam come over here. Her and I can chill in the pool. When you're done with Mike, we can all go out in the Jeep."

Shit. Think fast.

"That won't work Nic. Mike said that we're gonna be using all sorts of loud tools. Impact drivers, saws, loud stuff like that. You girls won't be able to relax with all the banging going on next door."

My cop bullshit artistry is still strong but my wife can usually tell when I'm lying. Luckily, she likes Mike and always wants me to 'make new friends' and 'be nicer to people,' whatever that is supposed to mean. Right now, I don't care because it seems to work.

"Ok my love, just be safe working with him. Don't hurt yourself. I need you for sweet lovin' when I get home." She says and plants a soft kiss on my cheek.

CHAPTER 14

There are times in one's life where introspection is unavoidable. A crossroads. Like many, I have had a handful of them. Some of them you know, or at least hope, are going to turn out great. Like your wedding day. When you're standing at the altar knowing that your world is about to change. You will be sharing all your experiences, financial gains and worries, ups and downs, and all of the rest of the cliché wedding day shit with one person for the rest of your life. Albeit a terrible time to make the decision, you can still run from that alter if you so choose.

A crossroads. Some can go either way, such as arriving at boot camp. You hope that you serve an enlistment full of great experiences traveling to faraway places and earning money for college. There is also the knowledge in the back of your head that you may die in combat. Most people don't have that introspective moment while standing in line at Home Depot. I look at the contents of my cart: a half dozen 'Homer' buckets, as many bags of Quikrete, and bleach. A crossroads. I throw in some impulse buys such as candy, a Coke, and one of those yellow flashlights with the massive six-volt battery to round off my purchase a little. I am quickly evaluating my choices. What should I have done differently? Should I have gone out to my driveway? Should I have just let him break into my car? That would be another gun on the streets. What if that gun, my stolen gun, killed an innocent? Maybe even killed a cop.

As I approach the cashier, I realize that I don't have any cash and need to pay with a card. Goddamn. I should be better at this. I'm wearing a hooded sweat, baseball hat, and sunglasses, all in an attempt to maintain anonymity and here I am about to pay with my own credit card. Like most Americans, I don't carry cash. Do I leave the line? Whatever, be cool. People buy this stuff all the time. I am not quite sure if I only think that or say it aloud as I swipe my Discover card as payment. The look on the cashier's face says that I probably said it aloud. Fuck. I should be better at this.

CHAPTER 15

I've learned a lot about my neighbor in the last twenty-four hours. He used to race cars before car racing paid anything. He worked on cars as a paying job and raced cars for fun when he wasn't fixing them for money. He had a huge amount of knowledge about all types of cars. It was a nice history lesson in automobiles. Exactly what I needed to distract me from the gruesomeness of the task at hand.

He also opened up about his military service. Not a huge amount but it definitely gave me a little insight. And given the current situation, I found his experiences to be very beneficial. Mike served in Vietnam during '67 and '68. Although he did not say it outright, I can gather that he took many souls during his time in war. He was an infantryman and saw much carnage up close. That explains his tolerance. He said his service in combat was for "God and Country" and would never wish harm on anyone that "didn't fucking bother me" as he put it. Turns out that one of Mike's trucks had been broken into, presumably by the present company. Between that and not wanting the commotion near his house, he seemed all too happy to help me. Well, that may be an overstatement. He just wasn't as put out as I would have been if it were me.

Mike's service in the military involved killing. 'Stacking bodies' as some call it. Mine involved saving, as I was a medic. Referred to as 'Death Cheaters' by some in the know. While both he and I saw our share of death and dismemberment, neither one of our military assignments involved our current task. But like one learns in the military: *adapt, improvise and overcome.*

Once my Jeep went rolling down the street, I immediately proceeded to remove one of the wooden 8' by 8' shadowbox fence panels that separate my yard from Mike's. He made the executive decision to bring our 'guest,' as we ultimately decided to refer to him as, to his yard. My yard is immaculately and minimally landscaped, primarily with light-colored paving stones. The wife insisted on hiring people to maintain the yard and pool so that negated the need for any type of shed on my property. Long story short, I had no concealment to host our 'guest.'

Mike's yard, on the other hand, has a thirty foot by fifty-foot workshop at the rear. I'm not positive but judging by the look of it, I think his shop was bigger than his house. In the shop is every tool imaginable, a car lift, a beautiful old Chevy, an engine hoist, and a half dozen fifty-five-gallon drums inside the shop and a few around the back. Those drums will come in handy.

When we bring our 'guest' into the shop, Mike spreads out a large tarp across the floor. He put weights on all corners to secure it in place and we place the 'guest' on top. Mike rolls over what I think is the largest tool chest that I have ever seen. That was until I look across the shop and see an even bigger one. He lifts up one of the compartment doors on it and pulls out a reciprocating saw, saying "You'll probably do best with the bi-metal blades." As he says that, he fumbles through a few blades in the drawer. "Smaller tighter teeth on those, like the surgeons use. Don't use the wood blades. They'll wreck the bones and make a mess."

Mike then goes and drags a fifty-five-gallon drum over. He then grabs a small orange bucket. "The big bucket is for him. Try to use a few of them. It will make it easier to break everything down. The small one is for you... In case you lose your cookies."

I look at Mike, "Break everything down?"

"Yeah, unless of course, you wanna go the taxidermy route."

Turns out Mike has a sick sense of humor. I imagine that I have a disgusted look on my face because Mike's next words were not minced in any way.

"Look, you killed this motherfucker, not me. I'm not here to judge you, only help. But if my help is not appreciated, then you can load up your dead fella and move along."

Well, he has a point.

"Sorry, I wasn't. I mean, I didn't. Um."

"More like you aren't. And you need to be. There's a tarp, cutting tools, and the drums. I have some lye and a little sulfuric acid. The Quikrete and buckets weren't a bad idea either. I'll probably have to get a little more but it will be a start. I'll come give you a hand in a bit but I haven't had my coffee yet. I'm going to go inside and pour a cup. You get started and I'll be out in a bit." Mike begins his stride towards his house.

I look down at our 'guest,' at the tools, and then at Mike walking away. The totality of this situation is really beginning to set in now.

"Why didn't you just call this thing in?" Mike says as he turns before exiting the shop.

"What?"

"I mean, you're a cop. Why didn't you just call 911? Tell them who you are and to come grab the body." Mike was completely serious with his question.

"If those days ever existed, they're long gone. A cop can't shoot a kid without it being a media firestorm. Maybe I should have called. Who knows?" I couldn't have put Nicole through that. And I'm not having my town torn apart by riots.

"Kid? Looks grown to me. Well, times changed I guess."

I don't know if there was a time where *this* could ever be right but here I am dealing with it. Fuck.

"Black or white?" The voice is miles away.

"Hey, black or white?!" The sternness of Mike's voice snaps me back to reality but I just stare at him as I didn't fully comprehend the question.

"How do you like your coffee?"

I glance down at our 'guest' and say to Mike, "Black."

As Mike turns around, he says "Get to work" and before shutting the door behind him he presses a button on the receiver. The stereo springs to life and the surround sound in the shop begins to provide the soundtrack for this task. Queen's *Don't Stop Me Now* was not the song I expected to play. I don't know what I expected but I really like that song and somehow, I feel as though I may never want to listen to it again.

CHAPTER 16

"Where are you at with that case?"

So vague. Every damn time. It drives me nuts. I currently have a caseload that is twenty cases deep and he has the nerve to ask me about *that* case.

"What case ya referring to, Sarge?" I know full damn well which one.

"Some lady left a voicemail saying you weren't taking her case seriously. She wants to file a complaint." He delivers the last three words with conviction and something slightly resembling authority; which is very out of character. For almost a half-second I mustered up a little respect for his rank. It didn't last long. He's referring to the damn Facebook Lady. I should have known. I could have an unsolved homicide and the boss could not possibly care less as long as his phone was not ringing.

"Hand her a complaint packet and tell her to have a nice day. It's a total BS case. It never should have been taken by road patrol." What I am really saying is that it never should have been assigned by him if he knew what he was doing. A Detective

Sergeant should take the time to read the report before firing it off to a detective for follow up. Filter out the bullshit. Massive waste of time; the case as well as the sergeant.

"Do something to make the lady happy, will ya? Write a subpoena or something."

"You bet Sarge. I'll see if SWAT is available to handle it. This is a serious caper!"

"Watch the attitude." He says as he drops a new case file onto my desk. "And look into this ASAP! The road just took a Signal 8 report. Probably a runaway or dope related but get on it now, please. For the family. I don't need to be handing out two complaint packets today."

And with that, another headache lands on my desk. I am sure he could feel my eyes burning holes in his back as he waddled out of my office. He is not morbidly obese or anything. He just has the body type of someone who couldn't describe the inside of a gym. Like a skinny fat guy. Little arms and skinny legs but with a fat face and gut. Like a rope with a knot in it. Only six years older than me; although you would never guess that we belong to the same generation.

Fantastic. A missing person case. No driver's license number but has an ID card number assigned. I don't recognize the name. I run the number in NCIC. Hopefully, there is a picture attached to the number. There was a picture attached.

I have heard stories during my lifetime where people reported being taken by surprise. Not like the military ambush surprise because in all truth, that is never a complete surprise. There is always a little part of you that thinks the enemy is lying in wait around every corner. Not even the kind of surprise where you walk in and find your spouse in bed with someone else. No matter how devoted your spouse may be, one always thinks that could be a possibility. I mean the kind of surprise you see in the movies. Like when an alien lands in your backyard or a relative from the future visits you. The kind of surprise that occurs when you get assigned a missing person case and see the identification card photo of the subject only to recognize him as the man whom you shot in your driveway during a foiled car burglary and had your neighbor help hide the body the prior day. The kind of genuine surprise that would prompt you to say 'you have got to be fucking kidding me' if you could only find the air to speak with. It takes your breath away. I thought that I experienced it yesterday when Mike approached me in the yard. Not so much. This was the out-of-body 'pinch me I'm dreaming' kind of surprise. Total fucking shock.

"How ya doing buddy?" The voice was miles away. Faint. From a distant cavern. The voice may have been speaking to me but it is unreasonable to expect a reply from that distance.

"Hey!" Still too far away to solicit a response from me.

The banging on my desk brings me back to reality. "Hey! What's the matter with you? You look like you've seen a ghost. You ok?" It's my 'work wife,' Detective Karen Mitchell, and she is standing in front of my desk. I look at her. Then I glance at the clock on the wall. 9:41 am. She's scheduled to be in at 9 am. She notices my glace and provides the following spontaneous statement, "My kid was sick this morning." Riiight. That poor little bastard must be on his deathbed because she always saunters in around this time.

"I hope he's ok." That is all that I can manage to piece together.

"I hope *you're* ok," she replies. "You were catatonic when I walked in. You completely ignored me."

"Yeah, sorry. Spacing out, I guess. Sarge handed me this case. So boring it put me to sleep."

"What is it?" She says and she reaches for the case file.

"Nothing. Nonsense probably. I'll look into it later." I place the file in the bottom drawer. "Perry and I are doing Giovessi's for lunch. Wanna join?"

CHAPTER 17

Two days. I haven't slept. Thank God Nic hasn't noticed. Tuesday. Garbage Day. I walk the can out to the side of the road as per usual. I see Mike doing the same. We give each other the same routine wave that we always do, except this time there is an added gesture. Mike points to an orange bucket that has been placed next to a coconut palm on our shared lot line. I look at the bucket and then back to Mike. He looks at the bucket and then to my garbage can. Fuck. I remember his words: "Don't put em all out at once. It will piss off the garbage men and attract unwanted attention." Ten minutes later I pull out of my driveway and head to work giving one final glance to the bucket placed next to my garbage can as I pull away. I hope it's not there when I come home.

"Hey, sweety." Her voice enters my office just before she does. "Your appointment is here." Shelly, the administrative assistant for the bureau. Assistant. That's akin to calling air the assistant to breathing. She could do my job in her sleep. Many jokingly refer to her as the best detective at the agency; although it's not a joke. If she likes you, you will have a much easier time in the bureau. If not, you won't. She likes me. "This one looks fragile. Good luck." She exits the room before her voice does.

"Appointment?" Asks Perry.

"Yeah. Controlled call for a sex batt case. Young victim too."

"Let me guess… Uncle?"

"Bingo." Not exactly keen investigative work on his behalf. Perpetrators of victims that age are often related. Disgusting.

"Let me know if the victim advocate is hot!" In what seems to be a trend, Perry's body is gone before his voice is and he likely does not hear me refer to him as an animal.

I go to the lobby of the PD and meet with my victim, as well as the victim advocate. She *is* hot. Young too, although that is not uncommon. Most victim advocates are young women who just finished their degree in some type of counseling major. They take this low-paying and emotionally taxing job as a resume builder as they further their studies. It is a high burnout job. How long can you be a shoulder to cry on for victims of sexual or domestic abuse without your emotional bank becoming completely depleted.

I guide my victim and the advocate to the interview room. I am always self-conscious when bringing a victim into that room. It's not exactly a warm and welcoming environment. It's not supposed to be. It's designed for interviews and interrogations of suspects. No one thinks to make a room just for victims when designing a police department. One table, three chairs, and a large mirror on one wall. Just like you see on TV. However, unlike television, there is no one on the other side of the mirror watching and taking notes. In fact, the adjoining room is filled with boxes and no one could observe even if they wanted to. There is a camera and mic hidden in the light switch for recording. Nobody ever seems to notice.

"Do you have any questions before we begin?"

Young eyes look up at me from a young lap. Red eyes. Glassy eyes. I move the tissues close to my victim. Tissues that I forgot to put in the room. Thank you, Shelly. I tell my victim that everything will be ok. Everything will not be ok. I tell them that they are strong and they can do this. They are not strong and I am unsure if this will work.

I have no evidence to work with and this controlled call is my only hope to build this case. I coach my victim but instruct them to not sound coached. I tell them to act natural. I am very aware of the unnatural situation this 11-year old victim is in. Most Hollywood actors couldn't pull off what I'm asking of this child.

"But I'm scared." The tears. The trembling. The body language. I was well aware of the fright prior to hearing it, but the word "scared" resonated with me and threw me off my game for a second. I thought about myself sitting in this room. What it would be like to be interrogated. A suspect. Will I be?

"Sir?" a distant voice said. A trembling voice. A scared voice. I luckily came back to the moment quickly. I see my victim looking at me.

"You're going to do great. You're very brave for doing this. What your uncle did to you was bad. You understand that, right?"

"Yes, sir".

Controlled calls present their own sets of difficulties. Poor reception. No answer when calling. Wrong person answering the phone. Another difficulty is the fact that most kids don't typically have conversations. It's usually text or 'Snaps.' I need the voice of the suspect. We start with a text: *call me*. The read receipts are on. Read. Responding. Response: *what's up kiddo?* The trembling gets worse. Trigger word. I'll ask about 'kiddo' later. Second text: *call me pls*. Read. Responding. Response: *now? can it wait?* Third text: *pls*. Read. No responding. Maybe a call is coming. Maybe the case is burned.

Deafening silence. No breathing. The trembling is visible but not audible. I sneak a look at my watch but it is pointless. Seconds, minutes, or hours. We are committed now. This call needs to happen. The ringer jarred us all like a thunderbolt. 'Uncle Neil Calling' displayed on the iPhone with a smiling male face. Not wholly dissimilar from the booking photo that I have in my case file from a DUI arrest in 2009. I look at my victim as assuredly as I can and say, "Take a deep breath. You'll do fine."

"Hel… hello." The trembling body has undoubtedly influenced the voice.

"Hey kiddo, you ok?"

"Ummm…" says my victim and looks to me for guidance. I face both of my palms down and pump them slowly as I lower them to the table. Whether calming or confusing, it achieved the pause that I had hoped for. I point to a prompt that was written down.

Looking at the paper, the victim says, "I want to talk to you about what happened?"

"What happened kiddo? Did something happen to you?" So far, not so good.

More trembling. That word is not helping matters.

"I mean… between you... and me."

"What do you mean? I don't know what you're talking about?" So far, still not so good. "I'm at work kiddo. We can talk later." Oh shit, I know how this ends. Quickly is how. Time to step it up. I point to the term that my victim said was used by the uncle. My victim shakes their head. Side to side. I nod mine. Up and down. I tap on the paper and give an expression that any child would recognize as a command to do what I say. Not the best technique given the circumstances but time was running out.

"I want to talk about our special time."

"What are you talking about kiddo?" With this statement, I put my finger to my lips. The same commanding expression that I gave a moment ago. Voice vacuum. This is a very useful interrogation tactic. No one likes an awkward silence. If you are quiet long enough, someone will speak. Even if it means admitting guilt. It is said that the opposite of talking is not listening. The opposite of talking is waiting. Waiting for your turn to speak. That's what we are waiting on now. For Uncle Neil to speak. Or hang up the phone. That is usually what this tactic produces via telephone. I keep my index finger on my lips.

After what feels like the lifespan of a Mayfly I hear it, "Kiddo?" Thank you, Jesus.

"Yeah?" says my trembling victim.

"We agreed not to talk about our special time. Remember?" Fuck yes. If nothing else is said I can work with this. A statement like this when played back to the suspect can elicit a confession. Even if it doesn't, it gives me probable cause to file for a warrant. If that gets shit-canned, at least he will be listed as a suspect in a sexual battery case forever.

I point to the paper. The victim reads the prompt. "I didn't like it." A moment passes. Voice vacuum.

"You know I would never hurt you. Right?" Glorious. Fucking glorious. I maintain my poker face and professionalism. I don't want to look excited hearing words that some therapist will be profiting from for years to follow. I only want this sick bastard to go to jail. I point to the paper.

My victim shakes their head. I nod mine.

"I didn't want to suck your penis, Uncle Neil."

And with that, I got the response that I needed.

"Listen, Kiddo. I have to go back to work. We can talk about this soon. Don't talk to anyone at school about this. Not the cops either. Or your parents. Just our special time. Talk soon. Love you." And with that, the soon to be incarcerated Uncle Neil hung up the phone. Fanfuckingtastic. Evidence of guilt. That statement will get the warrant for arrest and some type of prosecution. I'm thinking a 10-year plea deal. Nobody in their right mind would want a jury to hear that conversation. One thing at a time though as I still have my victim seated across from me. The tissue box is nearly empty.

You did a really great job I say. Truth. You're very brave. Truth. You're going to be ok. Lie. I walk the victim and victim advocate out to the lobby. I briefly speak with the victim's mother and let her know that I will call her as soon as an arrest is made.

The victim advocate, Kylie, stayed behind for a minute to speak with me. She looked very genuine when she asked me, "How do you think he's gonna be?" A myriad of scenarios floods my mind for the future of my victim. He will likely have great difficulty with relationships. Maybe a drug user. Intravenous probably. Definitely therapy bound. Statistically speaking, it would not be unheard-of for him to grow to become a sexual predator as well. Contradictory as it may be, early childhood victimization may lead to similar predations as an adult. I know all of the scenarios and none of them are good.

I look at Kylie and give her a reassuring smile. "He's going to be just fine. He'll grow to be a strong young man." She returns my smile, turns, and walks away. I watch her leave knowing that she is new at this and knowing that at some point she will wonder if I was wrong or lying.

I turn and see Perry's face pressed up against the glass door leading into the bureau. He's smiling and giving me a thumbs up. I know full well that it has nothing to do with the controlled call. I look at him and gesture to the door. Either he can open it for me or I can scan my ID access card. The card that I realize I left on my desk. He opens the door.

"She had a great upper *and* lower unit! Total package on that one." Perry's voice can surely be heard in the lobby, which was not empty.

"You're a fucking animal."

He furrows his brow and frowns. "Why do you keep calling me that?" I guess he did hear me.

CHAPTER 18

Examining it. Probing its every letter with the utmost of investigative expertise. The gentle curve of the writing spelling names such as *Fritto Misto, Radicchio, Fennel, and Olive Panzanella*, and *Pasta e Fagioli with Escarole*. If he put this much effort into his cases, his clearance rate would be much higher.

"Perry, what are you looking at? You get the same damn thing every time we come here."

Without looking up, Perry talks about how he would get something different if he knew what the entrees were. He grumbled something about there not being Italian to English translations.

"You know that you can just ask Alexia, right? She will tell you what anything is."

"Yeah, right. I'm a detective. I don't need to be asking some waitress what the name means."

I tell Perry to act like a detective and do what any good detective would do when faced with an unknown situation: Google it.

"You handsome boys know what you're having?" Alexia always seems so happy to see us. I can't imagine why. Cops are not exactly the best tippers in the world. That's an even more unforgivable trait considering the food is free here.

"I'll have my usual Lex, thank you."

"Boring!" Perry exclaims.

"And Lex, Perry will have a small Caesar salad followed by two slices of pepperoni."

Perry gives me a dirty look and scolds me for ordering his food, saying something about me not being his mother.

He looks at Alexia and smiles. How he can smile at her, I do not know. It's difficult for me to even look at her due to the fresh black eye that she has barely concealed behind far too much make-up. I've tried in the past. She will say she fell or caught an elbow playing basketball.

"Alexia, my dear. I would love a small Caesar salad to start. After which I would sincerely appreciate a slice of pepperoni pizza. Actually, two slices please." He hands her the menu and looks at me smiling. I can only shake my head.

"Whiskey yankee?" Perry asks me, smiling. It's his not-so-cryptic way of asking 'would you?'

I find myself watching Perry as he watches Alexia walk away from our table to the kitchen. This is the person who I choose to spend my lunches with. This guy. The guy that wants to fuck a battered waitress. I was supposed to be a famous baseball player.

I was a standout third baseman and one of Bucky Dent's best students. Now I am here with this guy. I think about mom. When she died, my playing went to hell, and dad left the reservation so to speak.

"I heard that you got a missing person case yesterday?" Perry was half looking at me and half looking at the saloon doors that lead into the kitchen waiting for Alexia to appear when he said it. I know he is not asking due to any other reason than general curiosity.

"Yeah, some kid went missing over the weekend I guess."

"Well, you know the great thing about missing person cases. They'll turn up one way or another and you'll get a case clearance." That is the common outcome. The missing person, usually a juvenile runaway, will end up getting hungry or tired or exhaust their couch surfing capabilities and return home. Or they are found dead. Either way, the missing person case is closed. I am quite happy for mine to stay open forever.

"Your controlled call went good earlier."

"Yeah, I suppose. I wouldn't call the situation good, but I'll put cuffs on the guy soon."

As I finished my sentence, Alexia dropped off two small Caesar salads.

Perry looks at me and says, "So?"

"Yeah, well I have road patrol trying to pick the guy up now on my probable cause. If they don't find him, I'll walk a warrant through to the State Attorney's Office so he gets scooped up."

Perry furrows his brow. "Not about that. Whiskey yankee?"

Jesus H. I should've kept playing baseball.

As the pepperoni slices are finished, Perry asks me for a favor. He tells me that he will be arresting a guy later this evening. Gives me the synopsis of the case. Terrible. A forcible sexual battery and sodomy of a little girl.

I look at Perry and ask, "You have PC to arrest this guy now?"

"Fuck yes I do. DNA hit came back."

"Then let's go pick this sick bastard up now. What are you waiting for?"

Perry looks at me thoroughly confused and says, "Now? We're on the little clock now bro. We can leave and come back this evening while on the big clock!"

"Seriously Perry? We're going to wait to pick up a violent child rapist due to overtime pay?"

"Like I always say bro: I'll solve any crime on overtime." He seems genuinely amused with his little rhymey saying. "But seriously, will you help me? You're really good at that shit."

Perry proceeds to explain 'that shit' as being interviews and interrogations. He refers to me as the 'crazy whisperer' and says that I have a knack for soliciting confessions. He's not wrong. I do. I do not enjoy it though. It is truly a mentally taxing exercise and one that is not quick when done correctly. I agree to help him.

"Awesome, I appreciate it. Come back to the PD around 7 or so. We will have him by then. That will give you enough time to eat dinner and fuck your wife."

"Easy bro!" I give Perry a look that he immediately recognizes as serious.

"Jeez, sorry. I didn't say that *I* was gonna fuck your wife. Aren't you guys going on vacation this weekend? The Bahamas, right?"

"Grand Cayman. And that's next weekend."

"Same thing. And the overtime you make tonight can pay for a nice dinner for two in the Bahamas. You're welcome." Somehow, he tries to turn this into him doing a favor for me.

Alexia returns to the table and I request the check. Perry interrupts and asks for a grilled chicken gorgonzola salad.

"For here?"

Perry smiles and says, "Yep. Karen is meeting me here for lunch. I'm working on that."

I throw five bucks on the table and tell him not to dip his pen in the company ink. As I am heading out of the door, I can hear him yell from the table, "Whiskey yankee?"

CHAPTER 19

I return at about 7:30 pm. Perry is sitting in the camera room watching the live feed from the interview room. He looks at me and smiles, "So? Have fun?" I know exactly what he means and cut him off at the pass. I tell him Nicole was out with her girlfriends and I had leftovers. Truth is, she made a fantastic dinner and we had delicious sex. No need in giving him the satisfaction of knowing that.

I look at the monitor. Closed body language. Arms crossed. Feet pointed toward the door. He's looking at the floor. I have my work cut out for me.

Perry says, "I have him all prepped for you. He's ready to talk." Yeah right. "I have you made out to be the good cop. You know I'm good at being the bad cop." How true. "This should be a quick one. He's ready to talk." Yeah right. He looks like he's ready to vomit.

I read over the case file and the probable cause affidavit. Now I want to vomit. I put my game face on and prepare to enter the room. The probable cause for arrest is solid; however, nothing secures a conviction like a post-Miranda confession. I redirect energy from wanting to strangle this guy to trying to get into his head. I enter the room.

I introduce myself. I tell him that I am a law enforcement investigator. I tell him that I want to hear his side of the story. As he is about to speak, I cut him off. "Coke or Sprite?" He looks confused. I ask again, "Coke or Sprite? Unless you prefer a coffee or a glass of water." He asks for a Coke. I return with the beverage and tell him that I am aware that he has already been advised of his constitutional protections. You never want to refer to Miranda as warnings. A warning implies that something bad is about to happen. And it is best not to refer to them as rights. Rights are empowering. I always call them protections. I tell him that I want to advise him of the protections again. That I want to clarify any questions that he may have. I tell him that I want him to be fully informed before we proceed with our conversation. That makes me look like the good guy who has nothing but the best intentions going forward. That I want to protect him.

I read each 'protection' slowly and methodically. While doing so, I nod my head and wave my hand forward toward my body in a welcoming manner. I ask if he understands at the end of each protection. "You have the right to remain silent. Do you understand that protection?" The nodding and waving have conditioned his response before his mouth opens and says "Yes." By the time I have read all of the protections, really warnings but I do not want him to know that, he has said "yes" multiple times. At the end, I extend an offering. A pen. The pen is powerful. People sign things with pens. He takes the pen. He's left-handed.

I say "Sign here acknowledging that I have advised you of all of your protections." He signs. At this point, he has been agreeable to everything I have asked so I move forward with the necessary line: "Keeping these protections in mind, are you happy to speak with me so that I can get a better understanding of why we are here today?" And so, it goes. Slowly. Methodically.

Rapport building. I ask about his childhood. He tells me that when he was growing up, he was a loner who rarely left his home. "So was I," I tell him. I wasn't. His parents sent him away to camp one summer. "Me too," I tell him. They didn't. "Were you touched by a counselor?" I ask. He was. I tell him that many of us were touched by camp counselors as children and how terrible it has affected us as adults. He tells me that he was raised to think he would be a millionaire. A movie star or rock star. Join the club. His feet are pointed toward me. His arms no longer crossed. Direct eye contact. It has taken three hours to get to this point but here we are. He finally trusts me. I move my chair closer to him. I look deeply into his eyes.

"The suspect in this case violently raped and sodomized a six-year-old girl. She was put into a medically induced coma due to the extent of blood loss and damage to her internal organs." His pupils constrict. "What do you think should happen to the person who did this to this little girl if I find him?" This is a question I ask during many interrogations. The answer will tell me if I have the right suspect or not.

His voice shakes slightly but he maintains eye contact and says, "I think everyone deserves a second chance." Bingo. I have the right guy. He says, "I think that maybe the suspect needs therapy. Maybe he's not really a bad guy."

I maintain eye contact. He looks away. I see a tear run down his cheek. I say nothing. He says that maybe the suspect wanted the little girl to feel loved. That maybe he wanted to feel loved. He looks back at me.

I look at him and give a comforting smile. I tell him that everything is going to be ok. I tell him that aspiring to love and be loved is a noble thing for the suspect to do. For him to do. He looks at me. I nod. I tell him that everything is going to be ok. He cries. We talk. I give him a warm embrace. I congratulate him for his honesty. I tell him that he is strong and brave. I assure him how better he will sleep tonight with a clear conscious. He wants another hug. I give it to him. He thanks me for speaking with him. He thanks me for understanding him. I smile and leave the room.

As I make a beeline for the exit, Perry put his hand up for a high five. I not so gently thrust the case file to his chest forcing him to grab it. I exit the building. I finally get to vomit.

CHAPTER 20

Christ. Nothing good comes from a ringing phone. Especially when the caller ID says it's the records department. The records department is the first place a person sees when they enter the police department. I've been unlucky enough to be out there to hear some of the nonsense requests made when citizens come in. 'I got arrested last night for not doing anything and I want the officer fired, right now!' or 'I got this parking ticket for parking in a handicapped spot but I was only there for like two minutes. Can I have this thrown out?' or 'I'll take a large pepperoni! Just kidding. Can I file a report?' Everyone is a fucking comedian. My sympathy doesn't run too deep though. The records people choose their fate. They knew what they signed up for. I guess we all did. I reluctantly answer the phone.

"Hello."

"Detective?"

I immediately regret my decision. They always ask like it's a fucking question. Yes! What number did you dial for Christ's sake? I want to disconnect the handset, walk into the records department, and throw it at them. At nobody in particular; all of them simultaneously would be my preference, if possible.

"Yes?"

I answer them back with the same queried tone that they gave me.

"Um. Oh, hi Detective. There's a, um, soldier here. Soldier? Oh, sorry. He says Marine. There is a Marine here who would like to speak with you."

"Tell him I have no interest in his yellow footprints."

There's a pause on the phone and I am sure that I can hear the gears grinding as she tries to process what I said.

"Um, yellow footprints? I don't understand."

You're not expected to you big dumb idiot. I didn't ask that you examine the content of my sentence, only to repeat it to the person standing in front of you. I guess that was an undertaking too daunting for you and a task far too great for me to burden you with. Some yellow footprints in your life would have done you some good.

I stare at the caller ID, practice some tactical breathing and say, "Don't worry about it. I'll be out in a sec."

I swig the last of the cold coffee from my 'World's Okayest Detective' mug, a present from my brother who has the same skewed sense of humor as me, and I head out to see what a representative from the United States Marine Corps wants with a local cop. After the week that I have had, I was hoping to roll into the weekend without any added headaches.

As I open the door leading to the lobby, I hear the familiar voice from a lifetime ago shout 'Doc!' and for a brief moment, I was back over there. I look over at the sound of the voice and am astounded to see him.

"Woody? Holy shit brother!" and with that, he and I embrace into a hug that few people know the power of. Not the type that siblings have or the type that spouses have. This is the type that only those who have shared the same life-changing and death-defying circumstances alongside one another have. This is the 'I owe you my life and I'll love you forever my brother' hug.

After what seems like an eternity, I grab him by the shoulders and push him away at arm's length. I look at the three chevrons and two rockers on each sleeve and say, "Jesus H. I guess the Corps will make anyone a Gunny nowadays!" and we both laugh. As I grip his arms, I can feel that they are as hard as stone. His chest and shoulders are bigger than I remember and his waist skinnier. Time has been good to Woody as he looks fitter than ever.

"And look at you, Woody. You've completely let yourself go. Doesn't the Corps have any physical fitness standards anymore? You're a mess!" I can barely get the word 'mess' out without laughing. Other people in the lobby are looking at me like I've lost my mind.

"It's great to see you too, Doc. You look good as well." And with that Woody brings me in for another hug.

I walk Woody outside for a little privacy and to enjoy the warm Florida sun. "I'm stoked to see you bro, but what brings you here? Last I heard you were canoeing heads with 2/6 in Marjah."

Woody pops to attention and exclaims "Recruitment duty sir. I'm here for the best of the best!" And with that corny line, we both laugh.

"Recruiter, eh? So, you decided to retire while still on active duty. That stack of chest candy and your experience and you go on recruiter duty?"

"Come on Doc. I needed a break. I put in to teach at SOI and ended up with this. I can think of worse places to be than South Florida though. It definitely beats Camp Lejeune. And plus, Darcy has family up in Fort Pierce so she likes it. You know the old saying, 'happy wife, happy life.' Anyway, how have you been? Nobody has heard from you."

"I'm good. You mean Darcy hasn't left you yet? Multiple deployments and she's still there? That must be some kind of Marine Corps record."

"Yep, she's been there from the start. Never wavering. She's my rock. And we're about to have number three!"

"Wow, congrats brother. That's great. And you know I'm just ball busting about the recruiter thing. The Corps couldn't ask for a better spokesperson. Just looking at you makes me want to reenlist!" That garnered his famous million-dollar smile that drove all the girls wild. This man's heart has only ever beat for Darcy though, and that only adds to the level of respect that I have for him. "So, what do I owe the great honor of a visit from a highly decorated Marine such as yourself?"

"Nathan Johnson."

And with that name, my world stopped spinning for a few seconds. Think fast.

"Who?"

"Nathan Johnson. He went missing over the weekend. I called up here and they said that you are the detective who is working the case. I was so relieved to hear your name when they told me. I figured if anyone can find him, it's going to be you."

"What's your interest in the case? Is he one of your recruits? Are you worried that you won't make your quota for the month?" I let out a little laugh with that hoping it masks the nervousness in my eyes. Woody doesn't laugh.

"Doc, as a matter of fact, I was getting him into the Corps. But that's not why I'm here. He's Darcy's sisters' kid. Nathan's my nephew."

CHAPTER 21

The United States Marine Corps is an extremely interesting entity to study. I liken them to fighting dogs that are chained up, barely fed, and mistreated. When you take off the chain, they will wreak havoc on anything in their way. They're part of the Department of the Navy but when you tell any Marine that, they will usually respond by saying the *men's* department. They are hard-fighting, hard-drinking, and hard-partying wild men that take pride in their reputation as doing the most with the least. They also take great pride in having been founded in a bar with the bartender being the first recruiter.

All Marines are riflemen, meaning combatants. Medics are non-combatants. It's not wise to go into battle without some type of medical support. Enter the United States Navy Hospital Corpsman. The Marines take Corpsman, never referred to as medics, and train them to hang. Corpsman assigned to USMC units will learn battlefield tactics, shooting, hand-to-hand combat, USMC history, and all the other stuff that goes with being a Marine. Once embedded with their Marine unit, the Corpsman will do through an array of other pre-requisite 'training,' non-sanctioned of course, to include: drinking heavily, getting into bar fights, being able to administer an IV while hammered, and generally protecting their Marines through all of that. When a Corpsman can prove themselves on the battlefield or in the bars, they will know that they have been accepted by their Marine brethren when they are referred to as *Doc*.

There's a saying about the Marines: No better friend, no worse enemy. I learned that early on. As a young Corpsman right out of 'A' school, my first duty was with the Marines. Not just any Marines, but as a grunt Corpsman with 1/5; 1st Battalion 5th Marines. These were some badass dudes. I didn't know "dick shit about fuck" as my gunny put it when I showed up, but within two weeks of arriving, we were headed off to war. September 11th happened while I was in boot camp. Here I was during the height of peacetime and looking to get some life experience and funding for my college when the biggest attack on American soil occurred. We were all told in boot camp, "You're going to war fellas." I was actually surprised that during that 'Don't ask, don't tell' phase of the military more guys didn't come out as gay in an attempt to avoid combat. Everyone seemed to embrace the concept of going to the Middle East to "kick ass and take names."

When I went to the MEPS station, I told the detailer that I wanted to be a Hospital Corpsman. They rightfully advised me that males with the Hospital Corps usually spend 60% of their career with the Fleet Marine Force. Not wanting to look like an idiot, I didn't ask for clarification on that. I figured that 'fleet' meant boats and 'marine' meant water and that 'force' meant a bunch of boats on the water. Little did I know that they meant the male Corpsman ended up in a foxhole with Marines. If I wanted that, I would've joined the Marines. I wanted to pick a job that had something resembling a civilian pertinence, unlike being the dude that steered a battleship. Maybe I would get out of the military and be a fireman, or go to college and be a physical therapist, or physician's assistant. I should've known something was awry when I got to boot camp, told my drill instructor that I was going to be a Hospital Corpsman and his reaction was, "You're going to be a bullet sponge." Shit, I had no idea.

So here I was, the new Corpsman with 1/5. I completely looked the part. High and tight haircut, in fucking great shape, and my uniform was impeccable. I looked to be chiseled from stone. Little did anyone know that I had exactly zero interest in being there. I was told to immediately get in contact with a First Class Petty Officer, HM1, and he would get me squared away. I figured that was good for me; another Corpsman, a like-minded individual. We would be able to stick together while among these fucking lunatic Marines. After all, we Navy guys need to stick together. A buddy system so to speak.

I walked into his office in the S-4 shop and casually said, "Hey HM1, how's it going?" I'm the new 1/5 doc."

"Get the fuck outta my office, you fucking fuck!"

So much for the buddy system. Judging by his next set of words, I can only guess that a bewildered look washed across my face.

"Do those big things on the side of your head fucking work or are you deaf? I bet you can get HBO with those fucking things. I said get the fuck out of here *squid*!"

Imagine my confusion when the sailor in front of me called me 'squid.' I thought only Marines called Navy guys squid. Here is a fellow Corpsman, who should be immediately taking me under his wing and guiding through the chaos that is the Marine Corps, telling me to get lost.

"But HM1, I'm here…"

At this point his boots, which were at rest and crossed atop his desk while he was leaning back in his chair, hit the ground with the thunderous sound of a howitzer and rocketed his 6'4" lean frame to a full and upright position. To say that his eyes burned with rage would be the same as saying that Hurricane Katrina was a slight rain shower.

"I'm gonna give you three seconds. Exactly three fucking seconds to get the fuck out of my office before I put my boot so far up your ass, the sweat on my knee will quench your thirst!"

As HM1 started to move from behind his desk toward me, my seabag and I were hauling ass and halfway down the corridor and headed toward the exit. If I wasn't legitimately scared for the safety and welfare of my body, I probably would've seen the humor in the semblance of the Full Metal Jacket type experience that I just had.

So, without being welcome at the only place that I was supposed to be, I went to where all Marines and Sailors without liberty or a vehicle go: The PX. Many hard-earned dollars get spent at the PX. Mainly on energy drinks, cans of Copenhagen, boot bands and socks, unit t-shirts, and Captain Morgan and/or Jack Daniels depending on your flavor. I couldn't even drop my seabag off because my point of contact for checking in, HM1, was someone who I was pretty confident wanted to kill me.

"Hey bro, who ya with?"

I looked up at the voice coming from above the shelf from me in the next aisle. Not wanting to make another mistake and end up on the hit list of two people, I immediately looked down at his collar insignia. I recognized the caduceus, the medical shield worn by all Corpsman, on his left collar, and the eagle and single chevron of a Third Class Petty Officer on his right, which was a rank that I had not yet achieved.

I simultaneously dropped my seabag, snapped to attention and exclaimed loudly, "Good afternoon Petty Officer" all while doing my best thousand-yard stare at nothing in particular.

"Holy shit bro, take it easy. Same team. Relax." He made his way around the aisle and found me still at the position of attention. "At ease." As he said that I relaxed my body and faced him. He had a look of confusion, examining me and judging by his expression, making the determination that I was an escaped mental patient.

"Bro, relax. You don't have to do that. In fact, I'd prefer it if you didn't. That's some serious boot camp shit right there."

"Sorry man, I just got my ass chewed by this HM1 and I didn't wanna be too careful," I said. I relaxed my entire body and hoped he wasn't setting me up for some type of counter-attack.

"Let me guess, HM1 Keinrich with 1/5?"

"So, he's *that guy*, eh?"

"Oh yeah, he is. People call him 'HM1 Kill-Wreck' and 'Das Furher.' Most call him 'RoboDoc.' Dude's fucking earned it though. He is a legitimate badass. You notice the scar on his face?"

"Yep."

"Apparently he got that from a bullet while in Panama years ago. Not sure if it's the truth but I've seen him in his blues and he has a Bronze Star, Purple Heart, and a CAR. I wouldn't fuck with him," he said as he reached out his hand, "I'm Geof. Nice to meet you... Pancake?" As he introduced himself, he looked at the name tape on my uniform and snickered as he incorrectly, but all too commonly, mispronounces my last name.

"Not exactly, but that version has seemed to have stuck with me for a while. All through boot camp, I was called 'Pancake' or something similar like 'Flapjack' or 'Pop-Tart.' Even word documents spellcheck my name to pancake. I'm so used to it now I don't even notice."

"Well, no need to make adjustments now then. Pancake it is!" Geof slaps me on the shoulder like an old frat boy as he says that.

Thank the lord that Geof came along because before he did, I was contemplating walking out the front gate and making my way back to Florida. He brought me back to his barracks room, introduced me to his barracks mate, a corporal, whom he referred to as 'The Snake,' and let me crash in a sleeping bag on his floor that night. Before that, we got hammered on Natty Light and played Halo for hours. Typical barracks life.

The next morning, he got up for PT and told me to do the same. He recommended that I go out and PT with guys from 1/5 and either RoboDoc will tell me to pound sand or I'll be left alone. Either way, he wished me luck and 'The Snake' asked if he could fuck my girlfriend back in Florida if RoboDoc killed me. I quickly found out how he got his nickname.

Geof turned out to be a really good dude, but I wasn't able to spend much time with him. I soon found out that I was going to the 'show' and he wasn't that far behind me. He went out to Iraq with 2/5, Weapons Company, and came back with some serious chest candy for doing some valorous shit in the field. He wouldn't talk about it but I read his citation and they make movies about guys like him. Last I heard he was selling his artwork in Seattle. Quite the transition.

CHAPTER 22

"You better fucking step it up, cupcake! I've got more time in the front lean and rest then you have in my Navy! Are you going to die out here? You can't die in front of these Marines! You're the one who they expect to keep them alive!" RoboDoc shouted at unhealthy volumes in my ear while running in formation.

RoboDoc would not relent. I was definitely regretting taking Geof's advice. As soon as I sneaked into the rear of the PT formation, RoboDoc saw me. He immediately crawled up my ass and found his happy place.

"This is the squid that slithered into my office yesterday and called himself 'Doc.' What do you think about that, Marines?" As RoboDoc said that, an entire battalion of Marines sounded off in unison. To hear that many Marines sound off really is an impressive sound, except when they are booing their disapproval at you. It's not how I wanted to begin my morning. It only got worse from there. The more fatigued I got, the more invigorated RoboDoc became. This guy would give Gunny Hartman nightmares. The guy is a fucking machine and if he didn't seem like such an angry asshole, I'd probably want to aspire to be like him.

Despite the thinly veiled torture session being passed off as morning exercise, I managed to survive. A quick shower and I was at the door of RoboDoc's office standing at attention before he arrived. I figured a 0800 hour start time was usual, and someone like RoboDoc would probably be there early. I was in position at 0725 and his door was closed. At exactly 0745, while at parade rest, I saw him coming down the hall. I popped to attention and waited. It was fucking eerie. I could see him in my peripheral but I could not hear his steps. It's like his feet didn't touch the ground. A sergeant walked by me a few minutes before and I could hear him coming and going. I was beginning to question whether RoboDoc was, in fact, some type of machine.

At a distance of about five feet away I sounded off, "Good morning, HM1."

He said nothing, did not look my way, and proceeded to open his door. I was about to perform my best facing and marching movements, and follow him into his office when the door slammed shut. I took that as a clue that he wasn't ready to see me. The lesson I learned that day was a testament to patience and persistence because at 1045 hours, RoboDoc opened his office door.

"Why are you still breathing the oxygen outside of this door?" The question was posed in a much more accusatory tone than an inquisitive one.

"Because I need to..." I barely got the beginning of the sentence out when he barked the following statement, "I'm going to chow. I suggest you do the same, just not with me. Have your ass back here at 1300 sharp!"

"Aye, aye HM1!" And with my response, he broke into step and marched off down the hall. I was confident that I could see his boots hitting the floor but there was no sound to be heard.

I figured that I would grab chow at the food hall in the PX. It was closer and I assumed that most Marines would be at the chow hall. I was very wrong. Lines were long at all options, but Ramones Mexican BBQ caught my eye. I will never understand how Marines maintain their high level of physical fitness on a diet that consists solely of energy drinks, fast food, and dark liquors. I stuff a burrito down my throat, pounded a large Mountain Dew and was back at RoboDoc's office door by 12:30 pm, a solid 30 minutes before he said to be there. Within 90 seconds of planting my feet near his door, I saw, of course not heard, RoboDoc coming down the hallway. As he neared his office, I gave the appropriate greeting of the day and, in a serious déjà vu moment; he slammed the door a la my earlier visit. You have got to be kidding me. How long can he keep this up?

At exactly 1300 hours, just as he advised, he opened the door. As I was sounding off my greeting he said, "Shut up, get in, and sit down!" I didn't waste any time.

RoboDoc stared at me intently, like a detective in a bad movie. "So, you're the new Corpsman?" Again, having said it more of an accusation. I figured that he wasn't looking for affirmation so I kept my mouth shut. "You don't seem like a complete soup sandwich, but your head is definitely up your ass part of the way. 1/5 is no fucking joke. These Marines will eat you up and spit you out if you can't hang. You better get your shit together. Pre-deployment workups begin Monday. Geronimo is headed to the big show in three weeks." He looked at the relic on his left wrist. That watch also looked like it had more time in the push-up position than I had in the Navy. Looking back at me he says, "It's 1305 hours. I expect you to be fully checked in by the end of the day." What the fuck? My check-in paperwork was barely started and now he expects it done by the end of the day on a Friday. I've been in the military long enough to know that most troops wrap it up early before they head into their weekend. I have maybe two hours to do two days of checking in. "Also, you're a fucking *pecker checker*. A *chancre mechanic*. You're not a *Doc* until your Marines bestow that title upon you. You don't give it to yourself. You earn it."

Just as I was about to speak, he shouted with a roar typically reserved for low flying aircraft, "WOODSIDE!" Quick and hard footsteps could be heard sprinting down the hallway and closing the distance fast. I wondered if RoboCop made any noise when running.

"Reporting as ordered Doc!" shouted a young black Marine, often referred to as a 'dark green Marines' within the Corps but probably no longer as political correctness has overflowed into the military. Completely rigid in the doorway, with a uniform as perfectly pressed as anything I'd ever seen. Handsome fella and looked to be in peak physical condition. I did look like a soup sandwich compared to this guy. He was very squared away.

"This is Lance Corporal Woodside. He will be your roommate. I suggest you listen to everything he tells you and you try to emulate him as much as possible. I am confident that he will go to great lengths to un-fuck you as best as possible." I wasn't sure if I was meant to thank him at this point so I just managed a nod to RoboDoc.

RoboDoc looked at the Marine. "Woody!" he said.

"Yes, Doc." as he maintained rigidity and his one-thousand-yard stare.

"This is the new Corpsman. Apparently, everyone already calls him *Pancake*." Jesus H., thanks a lot, Geof. That didn't take long. "Do your best to get him squared away today, this weekend and ready for Monday. If he is fucked up come Monday, then I will consider you equally as fucked up."

"Aye aye, Doc." Woody sounded off.

RoboDoc looked back at me, squinting slightly before he said, "Why in the fuck are you still fucking here?" As much as I wanted to appreciate his gratuitous use of the 'f-word,' I also believed in self-preservation so I evacuated the chair as quickly as possible as Woodside did an about-face. Woodside marched quickly down the hallway with me behind him, turning at a corner and ducking into an office. He then stopped, turned around and said, "Hey Doc, I'm Woody. Nice to meet you." He reached out his hand and I very suspiciously extended mine for a shake.

"But I thought that HM1 said I wasn't going to be called 'Doc' until I earned it." I was convinced that this was a trick and that RoboDoc was going to fast-rope from a ceiling tile and punch me in the face.

Woody laughed and said, "Kill-Wreck? That guy is a lunatic. Don't get me wrong, we all know he's as badass as they come but

he definitely has some screws loose. Listen, you enlisted as a
Corpsman and you're here to save my ass on the battlefield.
You're not a fat ass and you survived PT this morning with Kill-
Wreck riding your jock the entire time. Unless you fuck it up
somewhere along the line, you're 'Doc' to me." His smile seemed
as genuine as I'd ever seen and I immediately liked Woody. "Plus,
I'm not going to call you 'Pancake'" as he laughed.

"Everyone mispronounces my name. It's actually
pronounced…"

"'Doc'. Yeah, I know. We already established that." Woody's
smile hadn't left his face.

"We have a lot of shit to get squared away and not much time.
Kill-Wreck fucked you on purpose to see how you manage.
Lucky for you, your boy Woody is the Commandant of the LCU!"

I looked at him confused and he correctly interpreted that look.

"The Lance Corporal Underground. Don't worry, I got you
bro. As long as you like JD and Halo, we'll get along fine."

That was music to my ears. Woody was a guy that made shit
happen and someone that everyone liked. I'd never met anyone
like him before. Fitter than anyone I'd ever seen. He'd make a
game out of physical fitness. As handsome as they come. Girls
would flock to this guy, but he was completely devoted to his
high-school sweetheart. Extremely smart, working on his degree
in psychology, but also with the common sense and street survival
skills that were earned as a youth growing up in Atlanta. Woody
was a solid dude.

It turns out that Woody, and his LCU, got me all checked-in
by the end of the day on that Friday. It even included me wasting

some time going to various offices trying to obtain an 'ID Ten TANGO' form. That got plenty of laughs but did allow me to acquaint myself with the base. The weekend was spent working out, playing co-op Halo marathons in the barracks and drinking excessive amounts of JD. I managed to score some IV bags from the BAS and that served me very well in earning the trust of a few of my Marines that weekend.

Woody and I became fast friends, spending a lot of time together during the pre-deployment workups. He was well-respected by the other Marines, which helped me get some street cred. Within a few weeks, we were headed to 'The Sandbox' where our lives would change forever and my respect, admiration, and love for Woody and my Marines would be solidified. 1/5 was bringing the fight to Fallujah, raining hellfire against the enemy and I was trying my best to keep up, stay alive and not show my fear.

CHAPTER 23

River Mountain was a helluva Marine bar. Situated right in the heart of Kin, just outside the main gate of Camp Hansen, was the favorite watering hole for young Marines. River Mountain had a bottle of Jack Daniels. And I mean a *bottle*. Once that bottle was empty, they filled it back up with some brown liquor, presumably and hopefully whiskey of some type, and put the bottle of JD back behind the bar. The label had seen better days and I'm pretty sure it had more time behind that bar than I did in the Navy.

Woody had a big grin on his face when he said, "Whaddya think, Doc?"

I looked around, smiled and looked at him. "It's a complete shithole. I love it!"

Woody came to Oki about four months before I did, having been assigned to the 31st MEU. I came out here as the new Corpsman with the 7th Communications Battalion, affectionately nicknamed '7th Crime.' Woody was a lot of the reason I picked duty on Okinawa. Staying in Pendleton meant another trip to the sandbox, as did Lejeune. If I was to choose, which I was, I had enough hate and discontent for a little while. I sure as hell wasn't taking some duty at a Navy hospital somewhere. I would slit my wrists the right way if I had to do that. He told me that Oki wasn't as bad as some Marines made it out to be, especially if you were an NCO. After Iraq, Woody made corporal and I recently picked up petty officer third class. That meant better libo, off-base liberty, and the possibility of getting a car. So, I put in for duty with the III MEF and here I was, not only on Oki with Woody but on the same base.

"So, you're a fucking pecker checker!" said a voice a few spots down the bar and not at all posed as a question.

"No matter what your complaint is, I'm not looking at your dick buddy. Who knows where that things been? I know how you filthy fucks are." I gave the unknown fella a stare and did a quick assessment. He's got the eyes. He's been in the shit. And he's drunk. I gave Woody a quick glance.

"Doc, meet Gus."

I look back at Woody confused and say, "You know this crayon eater?"

"Yep, Gus is with me at the MEU. He's an 0432."

"Holy fucking shit, a POG. I'm getting shit talked by a POG. This aggression will not stand man. The doc does not abide." I say with a smile knowing the power of both references.

At the sound of the word POG, Gus nearly came across two barstools to hit me but the Big Lebowski mention immediately calmed him down. "You're lucky you like 'the dude.'"

I wasn't out of the clear yet with his hostility and that was fine by me. I've played this game before. I was having fun poking the bear. I know how this story ends.

"Lucky? Why? Were you about to come over here and try to suck my dick?"

I could see Gus getting angrier. Not just at what I was saying but for his apparent struggle for anything resembling a comeback.

"Navy guys are fags." That was the best that Gus could do to which I immediately replied, "You would know. You've probably gone down on plenty of us. And it's not gay to get a BJ, only to give one." At this point, Woody is almost doubled over laughing and a few other Marines have gathered around and are egging us on. Gus is quickly growing more agitated. Surprisingly the bartender pays no mind but she likely deals with this on a nightly basis.

"If you were a real doc, you'd take a shot of Habu Sake!" says Gus.

I glance over at the bottle behind the bar and examine the large snake inside coiled at the bottom, fangs drawn. I try to suppress the chill going down my spine at the thought of drinking that. I look up at the sign above the half-empty bottle that reads 'Habu Shots! $4.' Jesus H., people actually drink that stuff. There is no way that I am putting that stuff inside my body. No way. Think fast.

I know what is supposed to happen next. What this entire act is leading to. I help to expedite the process by saying the following, "Actually, if I was a real doc, I'd take that snake out of the bottle and shove it straight up your ass. But, then again, you'd probably enjoy that."

And with that, the fight is on. Gus sprung his body from his barstool and into my direction. I quickly launched my defense, a stiff left jab that grazed his head, knocking his hat off, but it failed to slow his assault. Gus drove his head and shoulder into me, driving me off my feet causing us both to hit the ground with his body landing on top of mine. I don't know if the wind was knocked out of me by him or the ground but nevertheless, I had no air in my lungs. As Gus was trying to impose his will onto me using his body weight and strength and trying to drive my body through the floorboards, I was countering that with a series of quick punches to each side of his body. Nothing devastating but repeated blows to the ribs gets annoying after a while. My punches got the desired effect as Gus raised his body off of mine and into the mount position. Not a good place for me to be but with his level of drunkenness, I was sure I would soon take an advantageous position. Gus raised his right fist all the way back to left field and sent it traveling quickly to my face. Perfect. He put all his momentum into that punch which allowed me to buck my hips up halfway through its descent. That sent Gus reeling forward in a nearly uncontrolled descent to the floor. With a quick wrap of an arm and twist of my body, I was on top of Gus in what is known in Brazilian jiu-jitsu circles as the guard position. There was a roar from the crowd of onlookers as I flipped the script on this Marine. As I pulled my hand into a fist and drew back for a punch, I could hear Woody's voice. He was ordering a drink. My priorities quickly aligned and I shouted to Woody, "Order me a Jack and Coke, fucko."

My pause caused Gus to reach up and grab my hair, pulling me down. I immediately regretted having a Navy regulation haircut long enough to grasp. He pulled me down onto my side and head-butted me. I don't think that was intentional because it seemed to cause him as much pain as it did me. Eventually, a barstool fell over onto us causing us to be showered by a few near-empty drinks as well as the remnants of an ashtray.

Five minutes later, Gus and I were sitting at the bar and I was still shaking cigarette ash from my hair. Gus was rubbing his temple but for the most part, we were both pretty unscathed.

I looked at Gus and said, "So, we doing that shot of Habu Sake or what?"

A disgusted look washed over Gus's face as he exclaimed, "Fuck no! That shit is toxic!" We both laughed. "Doc, you're alright for a Navy guy." That's how many friendships begin in the military and Gus and I would become good drinking buddies after that. Gus, Woody, and I solidified the experience with a snakebite shot, probably just as disgusting as a shot of Habu Sake but nowhere near as intimidating.

"So Woody, this is how you guys get down here in Kinville?"

"Pretty much. Taco rice and drinking at this place. Throw a tattoo in and you have the full Kintown experience." A sly smile crept across Woody's face and he glanced at Gus before looking back at me and saying, "Tomorrow night, we'll bring you to the 'Banana Show.'"

"The Banana Show? Something tells me that I'm not going to like it."

Gus laughs and says, "Like it? Maybe. Forget it? Never! Just don't eat the banana Doc!"

CHAPTER 24

Okinawa has some of the best scuba diving in the world. Growing up in South Florida, I'd been diving the east coast reefs, the Bahamas, and the Florida Keys most of my life. Southern California may have some beautiful beaches, and women, but there was no way I was diving in those waters. Ice cold and a feeding ground for great white sharks. I was happy to be in the warm subtropical waters of Oki to get some diving in. The same could not be said for Woody. After a few weeks in Oki and learning some of the dive sites, I decided to talk Woody into joining me.

"Come on bro, it will be fun."

"Fun for who, the sharks?" Said Woody.

"There are no sharks in Okinawa. It's a proven fact." I try to say with my most convincing scientist voice.

"You're a proven bull-shitter! Where there's water, there's sharks!"

"Come on Woodrow. You can start a trend. You can be the first black scuba diver on the island."

"There's a reason black folks don't get bitten by sharks. We don't do dumb shit like swim in the ocean. That's why God created swimming pools. You'll never hear about a black dude dying while climbing Mount Everest, or hang gliding, or any of that other crazy ass shit you white people do for *fun*." He was sure to put the emphasis on fun.

"Come on Woods. You can't be an 'iron duck' your whole life."

That hit a nerve and I knew it would. Woody was an absolute stud with physical fitness. He could run faster than anyone. He could do more pull-ups, push-ups, or sit-ups than anyone. Nobody could gas him out during MCMAP. But he couldn't swim. I used to call what he did 'controlled drowning' because he managed to pass the absolute basic requirement in boot camp but that was the extent of his waterborne capabilities. I knew he had aspirations for recon but without being a fish in the water, he was outta luck with that dream.

"You saying scuba will make me a better swimmer?" Woody asked with a doubtful look.

"Nope, not saying that at all."

"Then why the hell bother?"

"Because it won't directly make you a better swimmer, but it will make you more comfortable in the water. And being more comfortable in the water will make you a better swimmer. That and you'll get to experience just how amazing and peaceful the underwater world is. And I don't have anyone else that I wanna dive with, so I won't take no for an answer. At least give it a try."

That afternoon I managed to get Woody to do a shore dive from Sunabe Seawall. The seawall might be the friendliest beginner scuba spot on the entire island. Shallow and forgiving with some amazing reefs and marine life, you really won't be disappointed. Although watching Woody enter the water was like watching a newborn deer take their first steps, once he got somewhat acclimated, he wasn't that terrible. Luckily, I brought plenty of tanks because Woody burned through his first tank of air, about fifty minutes' worth, in just shy of ten minutes. That's called an 'air hog' in the scuba world. By the end of his third dive, there was nothing I could do to remove the smile from his face. I could tell that he was hooked.

"Doc, you're the fucking man! That was a blast!" Woody kept going on and on about all the fish he saw during the dive the entire ride back to base. During the dive, I made sure to guide him in the right direction so he 'found' the Buddha statue that is submerged in about twenty feet of water. He was so happy and said he was probably the first person to ever view it.

"Maybe the first black dude to ever see it."

"Whatever. Without me, you wouldn't have seen it."

I could only smile when he said that. I was very pleased to have introduced Woody to the world of scuba diving. I was also pleased to introduce Woody to one of the benefits of scuba diving. We were headed to River Mountain and Woody was going to learn how easy it was to get drunk after diving.

CHAPTER 25

The sounds of the firefight are deafening. My Marines can tell the difference between an M-4 round and an AK-47 round. My lack of expertise leads me to barely tell the difference between gunshots and explosions. Luckily all I was ever expected to recognize was the yell of 'Corpsman Up!' through all of it. April 10, 2003. I remember it like it was yesterday. The boys of A Company were giving hell to the hajis in Baghdad and I am hoping to Christ that I don't have to get put to work when I hear it.

"Doc! DOC!" I'd recognize that voice anywhere. It was Woody. Holy shit, Woody's hurt. Fuck. I jumped from the rear of the high-back that I was riding in and followed his voice. I saw Woody in a doorway calling me over and covering my six while I sprinted through a killing zone to get to him. My award citation would later recall how I 'courageously and without regard for his own well-being, ran through a firefight to render medical aid to a fallen Marine' or something like that. Truth was, I was fucking scared and looking for the quickest way to get to my destination.

I hadn't given a moment's thought about leaving my ass out in the open while I covered the distance.

The convoy was taking heavy gunfire from residential buildings and while the .50cal gunner was doing his best to turn two-story structures into one-story structures with the Ma Deuce, some of the Marines got after each house individually. That meant kicking in doors, running, and gunning their way through the building. I made my way to Woody and grabbed his arm saying, "Are you alright, bro?"

"Not me Doc, it's Hutch!"

I looked down and saw a blood-covered boot. I followed the boot up and in a pool of blood, I found Sergeant Randall Hutchinson. 'Hutch' as everyone called him was a small-town kid from Tennessee. He was from Duckville, or Ducktown, or Duckhill, or something like that. He was a really solid guy; everyone loved him. And he was a great fucking shot. He could put holes in holes at 300 yards with iron sights. And now he was dying right in front of me.

"Doc! Help him!" Woody shouted.

"Hutch, I'm here brother. I got you. You're going to be ok." I immediately went into what you say when someone is not going to be ok and that they are very likely going to die. The 'Ministry of Presence.'

"Doc?" Hutch's voice was weak but he was able to talk and that was huge. His skin was very pale and I could tell that he had lost a lot of blood. I began my trauma assessment of him and found that he was shot in the upper leg. Fuck! Probably hit the femoral artery. As I tore away clothing from the hole of the bullet,

I saw that there wasn't much blood coming from it. I tore away a little more fabric and found the exit hole with a finger. Hutch writhed in pain but I knew the shot was through and through. For a second, I thought that maybe he bled out already but there was still blood pouring from somewhere.

Hutch then painfully managed to mutter, "My gut."

I pulled his cammie top up and saw that he also took a gut-shot that was bleeding pretty good. I pulled him towards me and exposed his lower back. No exit wound seen. I reached my hand up under his armor and didn't find any holes. I grabbed my med bag and got to work on the stomach wound. An ABD pad and a large ACE wrap did the trick as best as I could. The leg didn't look like it needed a tourniquet, so gauze and an Israeli dressing were employed for that wound. I didn't want to burn through gear if I didn't need to. I figured I may be working more as the morning went on, and I did.

I reached up and grabbed Hutch by the face and said, "You are going to be ok bro, stay with us. Marines don't die." Now I need a litter team and a MEDEVAC. As I turned to Woody to communicate my needs, I did so in time to see him aiming his M-4 rifle in my direction and the committed look of a man about to kill in his eyes. I couldn't get the words out, only the thought of *Please, Woody don't shoot* when the flash from the muzzle blinded me and the shot then robbed me of my hearing. Light really does travel faster than sound. With my eyes closed and the deafening ringing in my ears, I was dumbfounded at the thought of Woody having shot me. Why? With a million thoughts running through my head, I was immediately brought back to life when I felt a thud behind me. I opened my eyes and looked at Woody. He nodded at me and turned around to cover the doorway from any more threats. Slowly turning around, then did I realize what just happened. Lying on his side with a machete loosely held in his hand was a man. There was a bullet hole in his forehead, slightly left of center. I stood up and slowly walked around this person only to find the rear of his skull had been quickly evacuated with Woody's help.

"Honey." Again, a voice miles away calling to me.

"Babe?" I ignore it until it is closer.

A nudge on my shoulder snaps me out of it.

"Hun, are you ok? What are you staring at?" I look up and see the angelic face of my wife. Nicole is everything I could ever ask for. Painfully beautiful and equally intelligent. She knows me better than anyone and for once in my life that scares me.

"Hey Nic, what's up?"

"You tell me. I've been calling your name for a few minutes. I was hoping you'd help me unload the groceries from the car and put some of them away. I was watching you from the kitchen out here just staring at nothing."

I glance across and notice the waterfall on the other side of the pool.

"I wasn't staring at nothing; I was admiring the waterfall. I'm glad that we added that."

"Really? I remember when we had the pool installed, you complained about the extra price. Now you like it?" Her bullshit meter is starting to beep.

"Of course, I do. It's beautiful and adds to the 'feng shui' of the pool" I say as I wrap an arm around her and pull her in close. "It was a great idea that you had. One of many. Like I always say 'wifey knows best,' right?" She doesn't smile and just stares at me. It's like she can read my mind through my eyes. She believes them to be the windows to the soul. I've used that line during interrogations but she believes it. If I could interrogate suspects with the accuracy in which Nicole can read me, I'd solve every case.

"You're sitting out here, in your work clothes, with a drink next to you, staring out at nothing. Is that supposed to be a one-finger drink?" she says while looking at my glass of Knob Creek.

"It was a three-finger pour in a prior life," I say with a shoulder shrug and a half-smile. That did not solicit a smile from her either.

Nicole and I have a thing where we will stare at each other, usually initiated by me, and see who breaks first. She usually loses and starts cracking up laughing and I waltz around like a proud peacock having bested her yet again in our silly impromptu staring matches. This is not one of those times. I know that I will have to give her something to satiate her. She will not relent without getting a better idea of what is going on. She knows me better than anyone and can read me like a book. I owe it to her to tell her something. Not everything, but something.

"Nic?"

"Yes?"

"Have I ever told you about Woody?"

"Who is Woody?" she says with a slightly confused, yet agitated look.

"Lance Corporal Woodside. Well, now Gunnery Sergeant Woodside. We were in Iraq together."

She walks over and softens her face. Beautiful, understanding and fully open to anything that I wish to tell her. "Babe, no you haven't. You really haven't told me anything about your time in the military, much less Iraq. I never want to prod but I'm always here for you if you'd like to talk. Who is Woody?"

I dive deeply into those big brown eyes. I could live there. Striking, compassionate, intriguing. She can own my soul with just a glance. I love those eyes. I need to be honest with those eyes. Well, as honest as I can.

"Have a seat Nic. I want to tell you about Woody."

CHAPTER 26

"Wow. That sounds intense. You guys went through a lot together." Nicole just sat at the edge of the chaise lounge chair and gave me a look with understanding eyes. She has such power over me. I can only imagine that she wields some of that same power over her clients. That is likely what makes her such a successful counselor. Until now, I never opened up to her about my time in service. When we initially got together, I had only been out about two years. She was much younger and was just finishing up her degree at FSU. She was not used to someone who always carried a gun and at the start found it concerning. She quickly learned my demeanor and came to accept it. I feel like I made her a little more vigilant about the world she lives in and she, in turn, calmed me down a little. When we first started dating, she said "If you ever want to talk about it, I'm here to listen" to which I replied "Ok." That was it. She never pried and I never opened up. That was nine years ago.

Now she sits at the end of the chair, having heard it all. Well, not everything.

I told her about boot camp, FMSS, the FMF, 'RoboDoc,' and Gus. She heard about 1/5, Iraq, and Woody. I could tell that she held back tears as I told her about how I wouldn't be here if it wasn't for Woody. I told her about Kin, taco rice, the story behind my shisa tattoo, scuba diving, and how Woody began as an iron duck but ended up being a great dive buddy. I told her that I left Okinawa to come back to civilian life in 2006 and Woody stayed in the Corps, ultimately heading out for a combat deployment to Afghanistan. I told her how I lost contact, kind of intentionally, with all my buddies from the military. She said it was probably a coping mechanism, and I said that I just wanted to leave that stuff behind. It was another lifetime as far as I was concerned. I told her that Woody and I got the same medal for our actions in Iraq and I told her what bullshit that was. She said I was a hero to which I immediately scoffed at and corrected her. Heroic is not how I feel.

"Woody is a hero. He saved my life and many others. I was scared and trying to not be killed, all the while making it harder for my Marines to keep me alive because of my habit of running through open fields of fire."

She touched my leg and said, "You ran through that to get to your Marines. They needed your help."

"I ran because the shortest distance is a straight line."

I told her about Woody showing up to the PD and asking for me. I told her how he somehow looks younger and fitter than ever. And I finally told her about his nephew. About my missing person case. I told her everything. Well, almost everything.

"Where do you think he is?" Nic asked with a concerned look.

"Well, if I knew he wouldn't be missing," I said hoping a little sarcasm would conceal my lie.

"You know what I mean."

"No idea. He probably got spooked and ran away. Stuff like this happens all the time."

"Well," Nicole says again touching my leg, "I hope he turns up soon and that he's ok."

I look at my beautiful wife and do something I have sworn to never do. "Yeah, me too." The lie hurts me. The truth would kill her.

CHAPTER 27

Garbage day. Another bucket at the property line. At this rate, I will have weekly reminders for the next month. It would be nice if Mike would put one at the side of the road in front of his house every week. That would speed up the process. I suppose I am not in any position to be asking him for favors. That I am in debt is an understatement.

I just need this week to be over. Leaving Friday morning for a quick trip to Grand Cayman cannot come quickly enough. And Woody wants to grab lunch this week. Fuck.

CHAPTER 28

"There's a name for those people Nic. They're called assholes."

Nicole does her best to hush me while suppressing her laugh. She loves that about me and I love that about her. We think the same way. The difference is that I will usually say it aloud. Like being on a plane that has first come, first serve seating. Southwest does this. Overall, I think they do a good job with their boarding practices. It's tough for them to control assholes though. You know, those people that will board a plane and place a bag on the seat next to them in the hope that nobody will sit there and they will have that extra elbow room throughout the flight. I get it but it is a super douche move. Those people have to beware of someone like me. If I fly solo, I will seek those people out and ask, 'Is anyone sitting there?' They are never quite prepared for that and, often feeling guilty that they are saving a seat for no one in particular, they will move their bag. I sit. This is especially satisfying if it is a row with three seats and they are sitting at the window or aisle and their bag is taking the middle seat. I will request they move their bag and I will sit in the middle seat and leave that third seat open. The look on their face is worth it. Those people need that kind of check in their lives and I will be the one to do it.

"Seriously Nic, look it up." I say a little louder "Google people who save seats on planes with bags for nobody. The title 'ASSHOLE' will pop up!" Nicole gives me a not so subtle jab to the ribcage and a wild-eyed 'Shush!'

It was worth it. My target got the message and the guy sitting behind me laughed. That's what I call 'two birds.' And deep down, I know Nicole likes it. She knows I won't put up with too much shit.

Other than the asshole, the flight to Owen Roberts Airport is easy. Up and down in less than an hour and a half. Plenty of time to drink a few 'Rum-Ritas' and get on island time. It's a quick trip, only two days, but Nic and I need it. I especially. My caseload can wait a few days. Especially since Woody stopped by. Yep, a few days without phones, internet, television, and the real world will serve us well. Everyone can use a trip to hit the 'reset' button once and awhile. Hell, we won't even have a car on the island. We're staying at a 'friend of a friends' place in West Bay, far away from the high dollar hotels of Seven Mile Beach. We hop in a taxi at the airport and off to a little spot along the beach that we will call home for a few days, only stopping once to grab a few bottles of champagne. Well, a few bottles plus a small bottle of JD just to be on the safe side.

Once we get to the place, a quiet little condo with an ocean view, we have some of the best sex we've had in weeks. A trip to the islands does wonders! Besides the postcard view that the condo had, there was a swimming pool, and a natural tide pool constantly being gently fed by breaking waves. A post-sex dip in the tide pool and we threw on some clothes. Typical island attire; a sundress over a bikini for Nic and some board shorts and a tank top for me. Both of us wore the obvious island footwear: flip flops. Not much different than South Florida dress but without phones or watches it feels adventurous.

A short walk up the road found us at home at a little tiki bar, Macabuca. We sat at the bar closest to the water and watched the scuba divers as they made the protected bay entry to dive Turtle Reef. This is one of those times I wish Nic wasn't claustrophobic and would be willing to scuba dive with me. It looked perfect. It reminded me of the easy shore dives in Oki. Just park at the shoreline, gear up and get in. Not like South Florida where you have to hire a dive boat at some ridiculous price to take you miles offshore.

My gaze at the tranquil aquamarine waters is happily interrupted by a nudge from Nic.

"Hey, I'm getting a margarita. You want one as well?"

"It'd be rude not to," I say to Nic knowing full well that the liquor of choice here is rum and not tequila.

"Lovely, I'll be right back." Says the bartender with a European accent. A beautiful blond hair and blue-eyed thing with a shape that would make most Victoria's Secret models jealous. Even Nicole couldn't fault me for looking at her.

"I'm no detective but something tells me she's not a local."

Nic gives a slight eye roll and says, "You are, in fact, a detective and it's pretty obvious that she's not a local."

119

"Well, I never claimed to be a good detective. Swedish?"

"No idea. Just because she's blond doesn't mean that she's Swedish. And please, don't ask her."

"Why?"

"Cause it's rude. And tacky. And she probably gets asked that all the time by guys."

"True. So, it's settled, you can ask her for me." I say with a smile.

"No."

"Meany!" and I stick my tongue out at her which she attempts to flick it while it's out.

Victoria's Secret bartender comes back with two margaritas, handing them across the bar to us.

I look at her and smile, "Thank you very much. I'm sorry if I missed it earlier. What was your name?" She smiles a row of perfect white, nearly blinding in the Caribbean sun, and says "Petra."

"Thank you, Petra. And I'm sorry if this is rude but my wife is curious and too shy to ask, but are you Swedish?" It was difficult to finish my question as Nicole smashed her foot down on my flip flop exposed toes. "No, I'm Hungarian but thank you. I think Swedish girls are beautiful. Any food?"

I look at Nic. "Conch Ceviche and the Jerk Chicken Panini please," Nic says to Petra with a smile. I didn't have a say in the order but that is long-established with us. I'll eat almost anything and Nic makes better decisions than I do. I'll end up ordering something that neither of us likes. I usually defer to her ordering for me so it has become a habit now. Petra flashes a genuine smile and retreats back behind the bar.

"You're an idiot," says Nic as she flashed me a look.

"I know. Cheers!" I reply with a smile as I hold up my margarita. My smile is returned by her.

The view is amazing and a few more divers enter the water. I am left to imagine the stunning aquatic experience that they are enjoying. In only a few minutes, barely enough time to finish our drinks, Nic, looks over my shoulder, smiles excitedly and says "foods here!" I turn to look at the gentleman who has brought our food out.

I hardly notice the sound of glass breaking. I just stare. Miles away I hear a familiar voice. "What the fuck?" I feel that my mouth is wide open but my body is too numb to do anything. The voice continues, almost too far away to decipher the words. "I'm sorry sir, he's a little clumsy." Clumsy? Christ, I hope not. I stare.

"Sir?" Stare.

"SIR!" Reality.

I can barely manage a "Huh?"

"You're food, sir. Don't worry about the glass. I'll clean it up. Enjoy your food."

I look at two divers exiting the water on the ladder that brings them up to the bar area. How did this happen? I was just in my driveway looking at Nathan Johnson. But he wasn't holding my gun. He was holding my food order.

"Babe? What the hell? Are you ok? You look out of it." That voice is closer. I recognize it now. Nicole. My beautiful wife. Did she see Nathan? Does she know? The facial features. Height. Weight. It all looked the same.

"BABE!"

I manage a look at Nic. She has a confused and mildly annoyed look.

"Did you get his name?" I ask.

"Who?"

"The guy who just dropped off the food. Did you get his name?"

"No, I didn't. I was too busy dodging the shards of glass from the drink you dropped ya big dummy. What was that about?"

"Sorry Nic, I don't know. Sausage fingers I guess. Are you ready for another?"

"I am but you'll be lucky if they don't cut you off."

Just in time, Petra comes over to check on us. "Everything look good?"

I smile at her. It was a harder task than it should have been. "Yes, the food looks amazing. May we please have two more drinks? I'm so sorry but I dropped mine."

"No worries, Dulian is coming back to clean it. Just mind where you step."

"Of course, thanks."

Dulian. Not Nathan. But it was him. Christ, it sure as hell looked like him. Get it together man. I glance over at Nic who looks almost orgasmic as she caresses the ceviche in her mouth.

"Oh my God, this is gorgeous. You have to try this. So tasty!"

I look at the dish. Then I look past the dish and past my stunning wife and I see Dulian approach with a broom, dustpan and a smile. Not Nathan. Dulian. He looks at me. He knows. But he can't know.

CHAPTER 29

The trip ended quickly but somehow not quickly enough. We stayed at Macabuca and got thoroughly drunk. At least I tried to. No matter how much I drank, I couldn't seem to catch a buzz. Nic got hammered and was so cute. She was having a blast, dancing in her sundress. We taught Petra what a 'pickleback' shot was and I should have got a laugh out of watching the two of them drinking together and giggling. Dulian left shortly after cleaning up the glass but I felt like he was watching me. I would see glimpses and then he wasn't there.

The same thing happened the next day at Vivo during breakfast. And at Rackam's for lunch. Nicole and I stayed at the condo drinking champagne under the stars for our final evening. Nic fell asleep in my arms in a chaise lounge. The moon shone brightly in the Caribbean night's sky and illuminated the cherubic face of my wife. She is so stunning. The light dimmed on her face and I looked up to the sky and saw the moon become hidden behind rolling clouds. As the clouds part and the light penetrates through, I am back in my driveway watching the moonlight in the white of Nathan's eye. I am in my driveway as he approaches me. Slowly at first but he closes the distance fast. I move. I try to move. I don't. I look up. Dulian and Nathan. Both rushing me. I reluctantly hold my ground. I try to but I'm immobile. At the moment they both reach me; I am able to throw them from me in one explosive force of action.

The scream. Too high for either of the men. No train horn. Just the scream followed by the sounds of waves lapping against the rocks. Nic. I glance over and see her crumpled on the ground in the fetal position. "Oh my God, Nic! Sweetheart. Are you ok?" She doesn't immediately respond. Just a groan as she appears to clutch her side. "Nicole, are you ok my love? What happened?"

Her eyes meet mine as she has a confounded look mixed with pain. "What the fuck? You threw me off the chair." I put my hand on her arm as I kneel by her.

"I'm sorry hun. Nightmare I guess."

"Iraq?"

I love her so much. I promised myself never to lie to her. I tighten my grip on her slightly and look into her eyes.

"Yeah Nic, something like that."

125

CHAPTER 30

"How was Cancun?" says Perry. He's cutting into his order of pepperoni bread. Giovessi's has amazingly tasty pepperoni bread.

"Grand Cayman," I say.

"What?" He doesn't look up as he dips a piece into his marinara.

"I went to Grand Cayman. Not Cancun."

"Same thing. How was it? Lots of hot chicks there?" Piece number two enters the marinara.

"I went there with Nicole." I realize as soon as the words left my mouth. Three, two, one...

"So, there was at least one hot chick there!" Perry says. I just stare at him.

"Aw, come on. Your wife is hot." Poor guy looks like he's trying to convince me.

"I know she's hot. That's a big reason why I married her." My words set him back at ease and pieces three and four enter the marinara. "It was a good trip. Short but good."

"Just good? I think getting rum-soaked and sunbaked in the Caribbean sounds like it should be more than good. If you wanted good, you could've stayed here and taken the boat to the sand bar and dropped anchor for a day or two."

I try to pick my next words carefully. "It was just nice to get away."

Perry puts the final piece of pepperoni bread into the marinara and looks at me. "What the hell are you trying to get away from?" He doesn't eat the last piece yet. He just stares at me. I should have picked my words more carefully. "Hot wife. No kids. Plenty of toys. I know you got cash put away." I think he legitimately wants an answer.

The night replays. Over and over. It's a looped feed in my head. What would someone else have done? What would Perry have done? I know he would have shot that kid too. Doubt he would have gone the route I did after. Maybe. I trust this guy. He's the kind of guy that would have helped me hide the body. That's a very in the moment thing to do. I doubt he'd be as understanding of the situation now as he prepares to finish his pepperoni bread and tuck into his chicken parm sandwich. Maybe.

There's no fucking way I could tell him. Or anyone.

CHAPTER 31

Tuesday. Garbage day. No bucket at the property line. Both his trucks are in his driveway. A brand-new GMC Denali. Full size. Beautiful truck. Not cheap. However, that truck pales in comparison to his other ride. A 1970 Chevrolet C10 in 'Brigade Blue.' Mike told me he bought it new after returning home from Vietnam. He says he is the "first and third owner" of the truck having mentioned something about having to buy it back after two months in 1982 when he lost it in a drunken bet.

I can only hope he realizes his mistake and does me the solid of throwing this week's bucket in the bed of one of those trucks. He can put it in whatever dumpster he finds.

I get to work and begin my ritual. Coffee check. I even picked up donuts. Not from Dunkin' but from the boutique donut shop down the road. They're twice the price but worth every penny. That's what the extra discretionary income from not having kids gets you: expensive donuts.

Fuck. There it is. The red light. I press the button. The British accent. "Hey Doc, it's Woody. I didn't want to bother you while you were on vacay. I found something out. Give me a shout when you can. Darcy says hi. Thanks for everything." I hang up the phone before the next message plays. Thanks for everything. Yeah right. I put my face in my hands and try to enjoy the little steam facial that my cup of coffee is giving me.

I stare at the red light. Who knows what the next message is. Who cares. At some point, I need to call Woody and see what he found out. I reach for my coffee. The weight of it is little more than the cup itself so a trip to the pot is forthcoming when I hear it. "Hey, buddy?" Far more cheerful than usual. And more bounce in her step than I have ever noticed as she saunters across the office to her desk. As she sits at her desk, she lets out a sigh. Not an exhausted sigh. Not a sigh that says *fuck this* or *I don't want to be here*. Those are the expected sighs. She lets out a sigh of satisfaction. Oh no. As she sits, I hear the unmistakable thud of a briefcase hitting a desk. Not any desk mind you. I hear a mug getting filled with coffee. Not any mug mind you. These two have never arrived at work at the same time. Never. I glance out of my office door and see what I already knew would be there. The eyebrow. Followed by a wink. And a sly smile. Damnit, Perry.

I need coffee. I don't need to hear whatever Perry wants to tell me. But I do need coffee.

"Hey." I ignore him. "Hey fucker, don't ignore me." I ignore him. I don't look at him. I don't look at my coffee. I know when it's full by the weight of it in my hand. As I walk away, I hear him laugh and say "They're built for comfort." This is quite possibly the last thing I need right now.

I call Woody. It rings and rings. No answer. Thank you, Jesus. I don't leave a message. I tried. I put my face back into my palms and enjoy my facial.

The cup is full but the steam is gone when it rings. Caller ID says 'US Government.' Fuck. He's calling from a recruitment office.

"Hello?"

"Hey, Doc. Aren't you supposed to introduce yourself or something when you answer?"

"The caller ID said government so I figured it was you. Either that or the IRS looking for money so I'd have some plausible deniability that it wasn't me if I hung up on them."

"Always thinking Doc." Yeah right. Woody goes on to tell that he found out from a recruit of his that his nephew was breaking into cars the night he went missing.

I say, "Really?"

He tells me that he found out there was one kid in particular that his nephew was hanging out with. A bad influence. Says he was with him that night. Apparently, he heard a gunshot.

I say, "Really?"

I ask who that kid is. Woody says that he doesn't know but heard of a nickname of 'Kodak.' He goes on to tell me that is a popular nickname at the moment and doesn't have any more information. I tell him "Thanks" and that "I'll look into it." Woody thanks me again for everything that I've done. I tell him that there is no need to thank me. Seriously. No need.

CHAPTER 32

"Corpsman up!"

"Doc!"

"Corpsman! We need a Corpsman over here!"

It began with a thunderous boom. An IED. It took out the first Humvee in the convoy. It was followed by the deafening sounds of mortar fire. I couldn't hear anything except what my ears were trained to hear: Marines needing help. That's why I am here. They keep me alive so I can keep them alive. It's time to work.

"Doc!"

I can hear the desperate screams for help but I couldn't find them. We were in an 'ambush alley.' The distinct sounds of AK-47 gunfire were erupting all around. The response of M-4 and M249G fire was swift and deadly. Hate and discontent. Destruction and death.

I could see muzzle flash coming from a lower window. It was a M-4 and oriented in the direction that I wasn't. That's a friend and he needs me. The screams were continuing from nowhere in particular. I ran into the house ready to render medical care under fire.

"Not in here Doc!" The Marine said as he rained hellfire in the opposite direction. I ran into the next room. As I entered the next room I said, "Who's hit?"

"Nobody's hit here. What's up with the Facebook Lady?"

I stand and stare at the Marine and he stares back. "The Facebook Lady. You make her happy yet?"

"Sarge?"

"Corpsman up! DOC!" The voices are shouting in desperation. The type of shouts that have echoed throughout battlefields for decades. I run to them. I am trained for this.

I run past the cubicles, being sure to dodge the industrial shredder, and into the next room. I stop and am stunned by what I see. "Perry?"

Perry looks at me and says, "What the fuck happened to you?"

I look down at myself. Covered in the Fallujah sand that gets inside of everything. Pockets, gloves, teeth. Don't oil your gun too much cause the sand will stick to it and make a thick mud-like substance. Don't oil your gun enough and it will jam in a firefight. I look down. Blood all over my boots. I can barely see the dog tag laced into my left boot. Wear one tag around your neck and put the other into the laces of your boot. That way if your foot gets blown off, they can identify you by the dog tag on your neck. Same concept if your head is blown off. There's blood all over my hands.

I look up at Perry. He's turned around and is now typing on his computer. There are case files piled on his desk. Without looking at me, he says "Giovessi's Later?"

"Corpsman! We need a medic!"

Confused I can hear the frantic calls for help. I can help. I am trained for this. I am trained to save lives.

I run out of the building and follow the voices. Rounds are impacting everywhere. Little explosions of dirt erupting from the ground around me. I'm a moving target, hard to hit. My basic tactics kick in and I hit the ground for a second. 'I'm up, they see me. I'm down.' I keep moving. The open area between the buildings seems to extend with every step. The screams are getting louder and I know I'm going in the right direction. I finally reached the building. It is completely shot out and appears as if one more round from a Ma Deuce will drop this thing. I enter.

Woody says, "Doc, you're here. Get to work!"

I look down at the wounded Marine who needs my lifesaving skills: Nathan Johnson. It's Nathan Johnson lying on the floor. He's been shot. I look up and see Woody and RoboDoc.

"What in the fuck are you fucking waiting for?" RoboDoc shouts it more of an accusation than a question.

I am in Mike's workshop. His 66' Impala is parked in the corner. It's a light yellow two-door with a 327 under the hood.

"Doc, help him!"

I drop my medical bag next to Nathan and get down on my knees. I look at his wounds. The wounds that I gave him. The continued sound of combat echoes all around me but I am now miles away. I open my bag. They all expect me to save him.

I stare at the contents of my medical bag. Bloody saws. A tarp. A bottle labeled LYE. I hear a voice and look up. Mike is standing over me and says, "Use the saws with the little teeth. They cut through bone easier. I'll be back with some coffee." I just stare.

I hear Woody's voice, "Doc, save him. Save my nephew. He's gonna be a great Marine".

RoboDoc gets down next to me and begins to yell in my face. I can feel his breath on my cheek. I can smell the Cohiba. "Well, dummy? Start cutting. You've been taught field amputations!"

I can't. I mean, I can't again.

"What in the fuck are you waiting for?" I swear I can smell the Cohiba.

"Cream or sugar in your coffee?"

"Doc, help him!"

I look down at my patient. The patient that I made. I slowly reach for a saw. Small teeth. It will cut through bone easier. I pick up the saw gently, as if it was a small bird and look at my patient. My hands are covered with blood. The sounds of gunfire are miles away now. I am trembling with fear. Woody can't know. He looks at me.

"Babe?"

I look back at Woody, confused.

"Babe? Are you ok?"

I am soaked. Wet and trembling. Woody approaches.

"Babe!" He gives me a shove on the shoulder.

The Monte Carlo Maverick ceiling fan. Brown. We have high ceilings and she thought it would look great in the big master bedroom. It is the first thing that I see before Nicole comes into view.

"Are you ok? You were so restless." She looks concerned.

I look at Nicole and give her a smile. She can't know.

CHAPTER 33

I like to think of myself as an optimist. Someone who always sees the positive in things. Someone who can make order from chaos. Take today for example. I woke up to seeing officers from my agency parked in front of Mike's house. They were accompanied by an ambulance from Palm Beach County Fire Rescue. Most people in my situation would likely have a negative reaction to that sight given that there is the body of a dead guy on the property. A dead guy that I shot in my driveway under the cloak of darkness and din. Nothing to worry about right now at least. I walk down my driveway with coffee in hand.

"Good morning, Detective."

"Good morning, Stevie. How's it going?" Stevie was one of the newest officers on the force. Nice kid. Not too bright but nice. I'm confident that I have more time on the can then he does in law enforcement but I can't fault him for that. I was once there.

"What kinda trouble you getting yourself into this morning?" I ask as I nonchalantly sipped my coffee.

"Do you live here?" Stevie asks gesturing to my house. I pause, raise an eyebrow, and stare at him. I then look at my coffee cup, my ragged Miami Dolphins t-shirt, my pajama pants, and my flip flops before I look over at the unmarked, yet obviously a police vehicle, car in my driveway and then back at Stevie. I say, "You're going to make one helluva detective one day, Stevie." He gives me a sheepish look before mumbling something about not knowing that I lived in "that house."

"So, do I need to waterboard you or are you going to tell me what's going on?" I ask.

"Signal 7. Looks like your neighbor died in his sleep last night."

Well, I'll be goddamned. This was unexpected. I leave my body for a minute and am floating above the property line that separates my house and my now dead neighbor's house. I remember hearing a saying years ago, 'two men can keep a secret if one of them is dead' or something like that. You get the idea. It was told to me by an outlaw biker. I was talking with him about a crime and the death of one of his club members. I'm pretty sure he probably killed the guy or at least knew who did, but nobody could get probable cause for the murder. Right now, I am wondering how he got rid of the body for different reasons than I initially wondered.

There it is again. Someone from another town is trying to talk to me. The distant conversation. So damn rude. Don't speak to me from the opposite side of the Grand Canyon.

"Detective?" Quietly and from a distance.

"Detective!" Slightly louder but still not effective communication.

"HEY!" And with the simultaneous snap of his finger in my face, Stevie brought me back to reality. "Sorry, I didn't mean to put my finger in your face but you were spaced out. Were you guys close?"

"Huh?" Is all I manage to utter as I wasn't quite computing the totality of the situation.

"Were you and your neighbor close? I'm sorry about it."

I always find it peculiar when people say 'they're sorry' when someone is dead. I know that it is a common and culturally acceptable thing to say but unless you are the one who is responsible for the demise of the individual, sorry is a bit silly to say.

"Close? No, not really. Nice guy though. Good neighbor." Fucking amazing neighbor is what I am actually thinking. The kind of neighbor that helps you get rid of a body. I can't imagine Mrs. Vincente on the other side of my house would have helped me cut a man into pieces.

"So, what happened? Is there a scene or will a doctor sign?" I ask.

I pray to Christ that Mike didn't off himself. That means a detective will come out and there will be crime scene investigators and all that shit. Even worse if he was murdered, although I think that would be highly unlikely. If that were the case, there would be a huge dog and pony show. I just pray that he died peacefully due to well documented medical issues and that his primary physician will sign the death certificate and no police investigation will be needed.

"There's no meds in there. No paperwork. It doesn't look like he had a doctor so it will be unattended. I think Detective Richardson is coming out to work it." The last eight words hit me like a mallet in the gut.

"Ok Stevie. Tell Richie to give me a shout if he needs any help."

"You got it, Detective. Take it easy and enjoy your coffee. Sorry about your neighbor." Stevie says as he turns around, adjusts his gun belt and walks back to his patrol car. The gun belt needs constant adjustment, especially for white boys with no ass like Stevie and I. I'm surprised the damn thing stays up around our waists.

Fuck. Fuck. Fuck. I am experiencing a seriously mixed bag of emotions here. On one hand, the only guy who knows that I shot a kid in my driveway recently is now dead. For all intents and purposes, that is a good thing. On the other hand, Mike doesn't have an attending physician to sign and Richie is going to work the case.

Death investigations in law enforcement go one of two ways. The cops will show up to the house of the decedent. This is often because some kid or grandkid hasn't heard from their elderly whoever for a while and they call us for a 'welfare check.' We show up and there are flies on the window, inside of the house trying to get out, and you know you have a good decomposition on your hands. Dear old grandma died in her sleep. We find a medication bottle and call the doctor who prescribed the meds.

They say that the old bag had a myriad of medical conditions and the death is not medically surprising and they sign the death certificate. No further police investigation, specifically detectives, is required. This is never the case for homicides, suicides, or overdoses. Any unnatural death gets the full investigative treatment. Every so often some old geezer doesn't have a doctor to sign off and a detective will come out to investigate although everyone knows there is nothing suspicious or criminal. Most normal detectives come out and do a quick search for any signs of foul play and then the body snatchers, I mean 'removal service,' come to take the deceased to the medical examiner's office where they figure out the cause and manner of death. When it's obviously not anything nefarious, that detective makes quick work of the scene and gets the hell out of there. Richardson is not that detective. He will go through the entire house with a fine-tooth comb looking for the shooter on the grassy knoll or whoever else he thinks may be involved. Fuck, I should've gone into the office on time today and I could've cherry-picked this call.

If I know Bradley Richardson like I think I know him, he is going to wonder why there are a half a dozen Home Depot 'Homer' buckets filled with concrete in Mike's workshop. To be honest, I would probably wonder as well. Unlike me, Richie will likely advance past the wonder stage and try to get inside those buckets. I feel most reasonable people, including myself, would think that the buckets are used as anchors. Maybe to hold down a tarp that's covering a lawnmower or boat. Especially in a yard as filled with random motorized 'whatevers' as Mike's is. Lacking anything else to lead one to believe otherwise, I doubt anyone would think that those buckets were filled with a mix of body parts and concrete. Unless something else was found, like a blood-stained saw blade or blood-stained anything else that I may have missed while preoccupied with disposing of a human corpse.

Although not much lye is needed to breakdown a human body, Mike didn't have enough. Plus, there was the issue of heating it up properly. Making 'Mexican Soup' is no easy task. Buying lye, I thought would be a little suspicious, and they don't have the pure shit in box stores. Going to some industrial supply store would probably get me on a terrorist watch list, so that plan wouldn't work. Mike was less than impressed with the bucket idea but I didn't exactly have the luxury of time to surf Amazon and get Prime shipping for some sodium hydroxide.

CHAPTER 34

I make my way into the office. What a fucking day to use a few hours of comp time in the morning. As I pulled out of my driveway, Richie did not even look my way. He was in full tilt investigative mode. This is not good. This is bad. This is... Oh, for Christ's sake. The lovebirds are canoodling by the coffee pot. I sit at my desk and put my head in my hand sans facial. I can hear some giggling as the door closes behind them. Good riddance.

"How is that case going?" Fuck my life. He doesn't bother to breach the threshold. He just meekly stands just outside extending his awkwardly long neck through my door. He reminds me of a prairie dog.

"What case are you referring to, Sarge?"

"The missing person one. Any leads?"

Leads. Yeah, as a matter of fact, I do. The uncle of the missing person is someone who I've known for years and owe my life to. He's made a little progress in identifying that there was someone else present the night he went missing who may be able to piece together the case. If not, I am confident that Bradley Richardson is going to crack the case wide open and not only solve the missing person aspect of it but likely make a homicide arrest too.

My stare redirects from the empty space where a steaming cup of coffee should be to the long neck with head attached that is partially obscuring my doorway. "No leads yet, Sarge."

"Nothing?"

That's usually what no leads mean but apparently, he wants a play by play. "The kid is entered into NCIC as missing. If any agency makes contact, they will call me directly. I made a BOLO bulletin and sent it to every agency in the southeast. He hasn't turned up at school and they know to call me if he does. Family is aware. So are friends. No cell phone. Nothing on social media but he wasn't that active to begin with. Right now, it's just a waiting game to see when he turns up. He's probably found himself a hot little number and spending as much time with her as possible."

He just nods and says, "Well, at least Facebook Lady stopped calling."

Yep, at least there's that.

I am the last one to leave the office and still no sign of Richie. As I near my home, I see his unmarked parked in front of Mike's house. The crime scene van is still there. The police tape is still up. I call and make a reservation. Then I call Nic and tell her to hurry.

CHAPTER 35

"Really? We're going there tonight?" She looks so excited. Buccano is our favorite restaurant and one usually reserved only for special occasions. It is not the type of place a couple on a cop and social workers salary can afford to go dine at frequently. The food is phenomenal, drinks are excellent, and it gives Nic and I an excuse to dress up and act like wealthy Palm Beachers. We both agree that the people watching is the best part. This is Trump's land. It's a veritable who's who and a car lover's wet dream to see the rides that pull up outside to valet: Bentley, Ferrari, Lotus, Aston Martin, Lambos. You name it and it's there. Luckily for me, the island police department is nearby and I'll park my truck there and walk to the restaurant with Nic. I doubt we'd ever get sat if I valeted that beast.

"Ugh, you know the people watching is going to be amazing! Remember the princesses?" Nicole loves this story. Three eastern European, we think, women seated in the cocktail area talking and laughing all too loudly. Never buying a drink. Not needing to of course. The wealthy men took care of that. They were all wearing boas. Each one a different obnoxious color to compliment, and I use that term loosely, their equally obnoxious dresses. The color palette was the same as those terrible Lily Pulitzer dresses the middle-aged yoga moms wear when they're done wearing their Lululemon workout clothes to go grocery shopping. I was confident they were acting on some type of reality television show by how over the top ridiculous they were being. Totally consumed with trying to look the part to the point where they stood out. That's not an easy task there. Nic was sure they were probably some types of baronesses from Estonia, or wherever, and I was sure that they were just gold-diggers. Regardless, we agreed on referring to them as the 'princesses.' That was years ago and we still talk about those women. I can only hope they found the husbands they were undoubtedly looking for. If they didn't, it wasn't for lack of effort.

"What are you trying to butter me up for?" Nic says as she gives me a sly smile.

"Honestly? I'm planning to get you drunk and take advantage of you." I give her the same sly smile back.

"You don't need to get me drunk to take advantage of me you stud!" She looks so sexy saying that as she bites her lip that I almost don't say my next remark.

"Oh, I don't mean sexually. I'm going to empty your bank account while you're drunk and live out my days like a king in Costa Rica!" I almost don't finish saying that due to laughter.

The sexy look quickly evaporates from her face and she crosses her arms and does that hip flare and toe tapping thing she does when she gets pissed with me. "Real cute. So much for keeping it sexy while married."

I pull her into my arms and give her a big kiss. I can feel her body totally relax. I'm lucky to have the same effect on her that she does with me. I release my grip enough to allow us to be face to face. "Hun, I was the same idiot when we were only dating. Instead of being your idiot boyfriend, I'm your idiot husband. I haven't changed. However, you should go change. Into something sexy. Classy but sexy. Let's grab some drinks and get some dinner. Maybe we'll get lucky and the princesses will be there." She smiles that smile that makes me fall even deeper in love with her every time, turns, and runs off to her room to get ready. That gives me a solid hour, of which I only need ten minutes to get ready. I go into my room, really the guest room but it is where all my clothes are, and I look out of the window. In an effort to be covert, I create an ad hoc urban hide so that anyone next door cannot see me see them. I see nothing.

Nicole is finally ready and we leave. I walk her to my truck making sure to position my body between her and Mike's house as an added bit of concealment. "Babe, I meant to ask. What's going on next door? I saw tape up and police cars. Is Mike ok?" Fuck.

"Yeah, he's fine. Richardson is over there for something. I don't want to get involved. Let's head out."

"Bradley?" Says Nic. "I haven't seen him for a while. He's always so nice."

Yeah, he's the greatest. I let her be the DJ for the ride to Buccano so that she is more into the music than the question asking.

Surveillance is an interesting component of law enforcement. It's tough to look natural and nonchalant when you're making a conscious effort to look natural and nonchalant. You need to fit in and not attract attention to yourself. You need to do what everyone else is doing while maintaining the 'eyeball' (having line of sight with your target). It helps to be unremarkable with the crowd, whatever the crowd may be. The big rule for working undercover is to never get burned. You don't want anyone knowing that you're a cop and sure don't want your target knowing they're being watched. That will shitcan an entire investigation or even get you killed. There are also administrative rules as well when conducting surveillance. Don't break the law in the commission of your surveillance operation. Most of us interpret that as don't get caught breaking the law. Don't drink booze and don't do drugs while undercover also. Any experienced narc will tell you that if a dealer has a gun to your head and asking if 'you're cool' with a line of coke in front of you, you will go full Tony Montana on that powder and deal with paperwork later. So, in reality, the most important rule is to not get burned.

"Honey, who are you looking at?"

I look at Nicole, look back at the guy who appears to be trying not to notice that I have noticed him, and look back at Nic. "Just someone I recognize."

"Really? Here? That's a first. Someone you arrested?"

"No. Don't look over there but I am pretty sure that I was in a class with this guy. I vaguely recall him working here on the island."

"He's a cop and he's eating here?" Nicole realizes what she said as soon as the words left her mouth. "I mean, yeah, we eat here but I've never heard of other cops who have."

"Well, maybe it's a special day for him and his lady," I say to Nic. Strangely enough, his lady looks a little familiar as well. Neither one of them has a drink in front of them. Even good surveillance elements know to grab a coke, splash it with water to lighten it up, put it in a highball glass and garnish it with a lime. These two only appear to have waters. I can't remember if they were here when we got here.

I get up to use the bathroom. It is at the rear of the restaurant. That allows me to walk past where their table is. Not wanting to burn myself, I use the mirror that lies past the sous chef and can see the guy watching me. Maybe he recognizes me and I'm being paranoid. Why would anyone from this department be watching me here at this restaurant? As I hold myself and enjoy my bathroom break, I take a moment to contemplate our earlier stop. Nicole and I always grab a preflight drink at a cheaper bar downtown, The Greaser, before making the trek across the bridge to enjoy a delicious and wildly expensive dinner. While at The Greaser, I saw a few uniforms sitting at a table having dinner. Nothing out of the ordinary, as those guys routinely patrol that downtown district and The Greaser does the half-off cop food hookup. Ask any cop, and they will tell you who 'does the right thing' with regard to a discount. Those guys had no idea who I was or that I was even there. Either that or they were the worst eyeball ever. As I give myself the final shake, I still can't help but feel that cop was watching me. Fuck it.

I leave the bathroom, walk down the hall away from the dining area, through a part of the kitchen unnoticed and out the back door. One would expect to be noticed in the kitchen, but the same Hispanic staff who works at the local burger shacks also work in the finest kitchens in America. They couldn't care less about me. Just another well-dressed white boy walking through their workspace. Maybe the owner's friend. Maybe an inspector. They don't know or care. I walk out to the road and look into the window trying to not be noticed. Damn waiter is in the way. Fuck. I look like a crazy person out here staring into the restaurant. I see him. Fucking dude is watching the hallway to the bathrooms intently. He cannot possibly know.

I make my way back into the restaurant and sit with Nic, who looks slightly concerned.

"Tummy ok?" she says.

"Huh? Oh yeah. Long line for the pisser."

"Hey, be a little classier and more romantic. Don't call it a pisser."

"Ever so sorry" as I put on my best wealthy old man voice and say "I was excusing myself to this fine establishments lavatory when I ran into Thurston and Muffy. Can you believe what they told me? They summer in the Hamptons. Can you believe it? What ruffians! Summering in the Hamptons?! So very tacky. I was going to offer our home in Santorini to them but I cannot fathom having underprivileged people like that staying in one of our homes."

Nicole is nearly bent over laughing, trying unsuccessfully to suppress it, all while shushing me. "Stop it, what if they hear you?" she says. "They'll kick us out."

"Kick us out? If they hear me talk like that, they'll probably comp our dinner and move us to a private booth! Anyway, how did I do? Convincing?"

"You're a natural at being obnoxious," she says while giving me a cheeky smile. "But the Hamptons are beautiful in the summer and very high dollar".

"It's all I could think of on the fly. Where'd they go?"

"Who?" Nicole says genuinely confused.

I look over where the eyeball was sitting and see an empty table getting bussed clean. "The cop who I recognized. He was just there."

"Well, he's gone. They must have finished up and left. That's usually how things work at a restaurant. I'm pretty sure that they don't live at that table." And with that Nic sticks out her tongue at me and smiles.

She's right. I'm being paranoid. They don't know.

CHAPTER 36

Luminol. You have got to be kidding me. I didn't even know that our crime scene techs had it. This is something out of a movie. Leave it to Richie to request it be used.

"As you can see in this photo, the Luminol reacted with a large area in the garage."

I can only stare at the projector screen.

"There is a large square area on the floor of the garage that does not react to the Luminol. Any guesses as to why?" Richardson has a smug look on his face.

"The killer used a tarp," says Perry.

Fuck you, Perry.

"Exactly," shouts Richie with far more enthusiasm than is appropriate. "You can see the reaction with blood spatter and drops outside of this square".

Being called to an immediate briefing by Detective Richardson did not fill me with a huge amount of joy first thing in the morning. He treated Mike's death with a thoroughness reserved for the most high-profile cases. The fucking bitch of it is that Mike did, in fact, have a doctor who he saw regularly. And that doctor was more than happy to sign the death certificate due to Mike's well-documented medical history. High blood pressure? Check. High cholesterol? Check. Pacemaker? Fucking check! Mike even suffered from issues related to Agent Orange exposure. Any normal detective would have hauled ass upon hearing that, citing 'natural causes.' Not Richardson, that son of a bitch. He has to do a walk-thru to check for anything that didn't pass the 'smell test.'

"During the search of the decedent's shop, a reciprocating saw was located."

Fuck.

"Luminol reacted on the saw."

Of course, it did.

Richie was up there detailing all of the different reciprocating saw blades that reacted with the Luminol. I could have saved him the trouble. Two bi-metal blades and a demolition blade. If he bothered to check the hacksaw, the Luminol would have reacted to that as well.

"You'll see that the Luminol reacted with a hacksaw that was located on a pegboard near the tool chest where the reciprocating saw and blades were located."

Of course, it did.

I feel like I'm having an out of body experience. I washed the blades off in the utility sink and wiped them down with bleach. I wiped everything down with bleach. Even the floor. The Luminol doesn't discriminate.

"There was a significant reaction of the Luminol in the sink located in the workshop."

I just stare at Richie. Holy shit, I should be better at this.

"Also located in the garbage can in the workshop was a receipt for a purchase made at Home Depot. The purchase included concrete and buckets. There were a few buckets located in a workshop. Those buckets have since been collected and reacted with Luminol and ninhydrin."

Of course, they did.

"Are you saying that there may be body parts in those buckets?" asks Perry.

Fuck you, Perry.

"Well, presumptive testing was done on a trace amount of blood located in the workshop. The blood was human, ruling out my initial thought that the decedent may have butchered some type of game in the workshop. DNA was collected and has been sent to the forensic biology unit at the Sheriff's Office for testing." Richie had a very dramatic pause before moving on. I am confident that he is a frustrated actor. "I feel that we may be on to something much bigger here." Richie looks directly at me. Maintain a poker face. He can't know. "Don't you have a missing person case?"

I look right back at Richie, trying not to try too hard to make something resembling a normal expression and response. I say, "I'm not following ya Rich."

He looks back at me intently and says the following, "Your neighbor may have killed your missing person."

Wow. My stare morphs into a slight and thoughtful nod. Richie. You may be onto something after all.

CHAPTER 37

"Did you know him well?"

"Not really?" I am suddenly very aware of the things that I look for during an interrogation. I am making extra efforts to not show any signs of nervousness and deception. My awareness is making me nervous.

"I mean, as well as you can know your neighbor I suppose."

"I'm very close with my neighbors. Our kids play together. We've vacationed together. We have keys to each other's homes." I just stare at him. Of course, he's super buddy-friendly with his neighbors. I bet his neighbors wouldn't help him hide a body though.

"Richie, I'm glad you're tight with your neighbors. Me, not so much. I prefer my privacy and I extend it to them. A friendly wave and a hello on occasion. That's it." I maintain eye contact. Not in an aggressive manner though. Enough eye contact to show engagement and sincerity. I think. Fuck, maybe it's aggressive. I look away.

"So, you don't go over to his house much?"

"No, like I said. A wave here and there. Think about Tim and Wilson from *Home Improvement*. Kinda like that." He tells me he never saw the show. No surprise there.

"So, your DNA wouldn't be anywhere in his home? Or his garage?" Richie is the one staring now. I think his eye contact is aggressive. Fuck.

"Yeah, maybe. You saw his shop. He had loads of tools in there. He helped me work on my Jeep in the shop before. We replaced the oil pan gasket."

"That's it?" Richie asked.

"No, actually. While the oil pan was off, we did the oil pump and the rear main. The rear main was easy cause it's a two-piece main and didn't require dropping the tranny." This is all work that I did in my own garage recently but it seemed to flow well. I have all the receipts for parts if he needed them. He can look under the Jeep and see the blue of the Fel-Pro gasket showing the recent change.

"No, that's not what I meant. Was that the only time you were at his home?"

I think on my feet quickly. My DNA and prints will be in his shop. Totally normal for neighbors. I tell him that I'd help him when he needed a second set of hands in the shop and he would let me borrow some tools. Neighborly stuff.

"I get it, bro. This isn't an interrogation." Richie tells me. It feels like an interrogation to me. "I'm just trying to put the pieces together. I have a few leads. The buckets are interesting to me. I have a call out to someone who will x-ray the concrete. Actually, they're going to do this thing called GPR. Have you heard of it?"

I shake my head. "Interesting stuff. Ground-penetrating radar. They use it to check concrete slabs for rebar, conduit, stuff like that. I just don't want to start breaking up the concrete if there's…" He pauses for what appears to be a dramatic effect. "Evidence inside. If you know what I mean." I know all too well what he means. Fuck. I remember the briefing. The receipt.

"Richie, I just thought of something. Those buckets." Now I pause for dramatic effect. "I bought those for him recently. He said he needed buckets and Quikrete." I figured Richie has already requested and seen the surveillance video from Home Depot. Either that or he will. If not, he will subpoena for the credit card details related to the payment. Either way, he either knows or will know that I made the damn purchase. Better to get out in front of it now.

He looks genuinely interested. "Really? Why did you buy that stuff for him?"

"I was about to pull out of the driveway one afternoon. He was pulling weeds near our lot line. I chatted with him for a sec. Told him I was going to run some errands. That I was gonna swing by Home Depot to pick up a few things. He asked if I could get him buckets and the concrete. He said he needed to weigh down some tarps in his yard to cover his project cars and other stuff. Sounded reasonable to me." It sure sounds reasonable to me now. Hopefully, it does to Richie as well.

He nods thoughtfully and stares. I stare back.

"What did you buy for yourself?" Richie says.

Fuck. Motherfucking fuck. I know what I bought. Buckets, concrete and bleach for our 'guest.' And a bottle of Coke, a

Payday bar, and one of those stupid fucking yellow lights with that massive battery that everyone thinks that they will need in an emergency and never fucking use. Fuck.

"What?" Is all I manage to say. Are you serious? That was my on-the-fly response. I should be better at this.

Richie furrows his brow and looks genuinely confused. He asks, "What did you get? You said you were going there to pick up some things. Surely you got something of significance, right?"

"Not really, no." Think fast. "I went to get a firepit. You know, one of the cheapish ones for when we get a cold spell. They're nice to throw a few logs in and sit around with a beer. They didn't have one I wanted so I just grabbed the stuff that Mike asked for. I think I may have grabbed a drink and candy bar at checkout. And a flashlight too."

"Not one of those big yellow impulse buy flashlights that are always at the checkouts, right?" Richie is smiling.

"Yep, one of those."

"You'll never use it." He laughs. I don't.

He seems satisfied with my answers. I can only hope he doesn't or hasn't pulled the video from Home Depot. I don't know where the cameras are but they sure as hell won't show me going anywhere near the damn fire pits. Before he leaves my office, he asks if I heard anything suspicious from my neighbor's property. I didn't. If I saw my neighbor acting suspiciously. I didn't. He tells me to let him know if I think of anything. I won't.

As he is leaving my office my brain doesn't stop my mouth from saying, "I didn't have anything to do with this."

He looks back at me and says, "I never said you did" before leaving my view completely. He's right.

CHAPTER 38

I sit and stare at it. I can see the high mark where it began. The viscosity leaves a slight trace. No condensation. Totally neat. I consider reconstituting it back to its original glory. It would be the third time. That consideration ceases as I hear her car pull into the driveway. I put the glass into the dishwasher and the bottle into the cabinet and take a seat in my reading chair. I would normally meet her at the door but I want some separation from the outside. Maybe that will prevent the obvious questions. Probably not.

"Hey, handsome!" She says as she seems to float through the front door. She's happy. I stay seated as she floats over to me. She leans down and the floral smell takes me away for a moment. For a moment I am back to our first getaway. Saint Augustine. She leaned over me then. Bare breasts. Floral scent. Warm wet lips pressed against mine. A scene that would make the hardest man melt with love and bliss. The Casa Monica. We were the only two people in the world that evening. That scent brings me there. Another kiss.

"Thank you for a lovely evening," as her lips pull away from mine. "Did you ever find out what happened next door with Mike?" Fuck. That didn't take long.

"Yeah, I did. Get changed and relax. I'll tell you about it in a few."

She stands up straight as a drill instructor. Hands on her hips. Direct eye contact. She says, "What happened?" Her bullshit meter is activated and I haven't even said anything yet.

"Nic, have a seat." She doesn't. I look away. I try to emote. I try to act natural. I try to act as if I am not acting. "Mike passed away."

"Oh my." Her stance changes as she put her hand to her mouth.

"Actually Nic, it's worse than that."

CHAPTER 39

"You have got to be fucking kidding me!"

Nicole has passed swiftly through most of the grief stages in less time than a person takes to drink their morning coffee. I told her Mike passed away and as one would expect, she was genuinely saddened. I then told her how Richie thinks that Mike may have killed a young man. The young man that I have been assigned to locate. The young man who is the nephew of the man who saved the life of the man she married. Shock and denial. Furious rage. I have only seen her as angry once in our lives. That was when her sister's then-boyfriend appeared to mistreat her sister. Appeared is the operative word as it was a complete misunderstanding. That was not known then and did not stop Nic from going high and to the right with targeted wrath toward the boyfriend. He was near tears. It's tough to watch a man in such a stage of fright. I don't blame him. I was scared too and she wasn't even pissed at me.

"What did Bradley say? What did he find? What does he think happened? Does Woody know?" All good questions. All ones I anticipated. All ones I rehearsed answers to. All questions that I had perfect replies to. A reply that wouldn't solicit any further questioning. Replies I couldn't remember when put on the spot.

I look at Nic and her glare demands some type of response. I respond, "Can I get you a drink?" I walk toward the cabinet. I don't look but I feel her eyes burning holes in me.

"No, I don't want a fucking drink. I want to know what the fuck happened next door. Next to our home. Were we living next to a murderer!" It wasn't a question.

I turn and look at her, a bottle of Knob Creek in my left hand. I'm right-handed. A cop is always taught to keep their dominant hand empty to facilitate grabbing their gun when needed. I look down at my empty hand. I don't know why.

"Actually, I don't think you need a drink either. I can tell you've already had a few."

Without hesitation or explanation, I say "Fuck you."

She is upright again. Straight as an arrow. Hands on hips. Direct eye contact. However, her face is softened and her feelings look hurt. Fuck.

I put the bottle down and walk over to her. My right hand is no longer empty. Both are full as I pull Nicole tightly to my body. I tell her that I am sorry. I tell her that I had a rough day at work. I tell her that I am as angry, confused and shocked as she is to hear the news of Mike. I tell her that I am sorry. Many times. I tell her that I love her. More than anything. Many times. I tell her to have a seat and I will tell her what I know. What I want her to know.

I go back to the cabinet. Both hands are full. I make drinks for her and I.

CHAPTER 40

"What are you thinking?" She asks him. She is genuinely concerned. She knows that he takes his job, his profession, very seriously. She has seen him fully immersed in a case before. His immersion is always active, rarely of concern. She enjoys the energy emitted from him while he is working an interesting case. She is his perfect opposite as she gives him the space and encouragement to give his full attention to his work. Many wives would be frustrated by a man who may forget an anniversary or birthday due to putting work first. Not her. She finds it all enthralling. While most teenage girls were chasing boys and spending their weekends at the beach, she stayed home reading Agatha Christie novels. As long as she has been with him, she feels as though she has been living those novels. She is the best wife that Bradley Richardson could have ever hoped for. But now, Tracy Richardson sees something different in her husband.

"I don't know. Something isn't adding up. When I talked to him earlier, I don't know... something wasn't right." His expression only added to her concern. "I feel like he knows something. I don't want to say that he is hiding something, but he was off a little. I can't put my finger on it. Is he protecting his neighbor in some way?" The question was not directed at Tracy but she tried to answer it anyway.

"He could be. Maybe protecting his legacy for his family." She says.

"That's the weird thing. This guy didn't have any family. I don't get it. He became so agitated when I spoke with him earlier."

"Maybe he is grieving the loss of his neighbor. His friend. Were they close?" Tracy asks.

"No, I considered that. At first, he said he barely knew the guy. Only a seldom wave. Then he said he'd been to his house to work on his car. Then something about shopping for him. It just doesn't quite add up."

Tracy studies her husband. His expression. His body language. Frustration is present but maybe a hint of denial. She put herself into the books she devoured as a young girl. She channels her inner Miss Marple and says the following: "Maybe he did it. Maybe he's your killer. It's always the last person you would suspect. You've read the whodunit novels."

Bradley gives her a confounded look, "It's not possible"

She returns a look of confidence, "*Anything* is possible."

He tells her that he has called in a favor to a friend at the crime lab who he is seeing tomorrow. "I'll be at the Sheriff's Office tomorrow. They have some new toys that should shed some light on this pretty quickly. I'll get this figured out quickly but I doubt that he's involved in any way." He looks to her and is unable to match her confidence.

"Remember," she says "anything is possible."

He nods. "It is."

CHAPTER 41

I don't remember the drive. It doesn't take long but I remember none of it. My head is killing me. I can't find my ID in my briefcase. One of the records clerks will have to let me in. The thought of that and the possibility of any questions they may ask are too much to bear. Not questions about anything of substance mind you. Just the usual nonsensical stuff. My throbbing head and minimal patience can't take it this morning. I just stare at the keypad thinking that maybe it will beep and the door will just open. With my briefcase in my right hand and the donuts being held shoulder height, waiter-style, in my left, I await a miracle for the door to open. And there it is. By either miracle or stupidity, my ID appears. Around my neck where I put it when I picked up the donuts knowing I would not have a free hand when I arrive to work. Fuck. It's going to be a long day.

I put the donuts down and brew a pot of coffee. If there is any day where I wish to be left alone, it is today. I bask in the silence and wish that it continues. I hope the donuts and coffee work their magic.

It's illuminated. Fuck. I have to address it. If I don't, Karen will walk in and say "You gonna see who that is buddy?" Fuck her. And not in the way that Perry has. Damnit.

"You have three new messages." Of course, I do. I press the number '1' to play the message, despite my urge to delete it before it even plays. Plausible deniability.

"First message," the British voice says. "Doc, it's Woody. Give me a call when you get in. I don't wanna call you at home and risk waking you or Nicole up. I got a call from a guy you work with. It was… I don't know. Just call me." Wait, what? Before I replay the message, the British voice says, "Second message."

"Doc, call me. This guy, Bradley, just called me again. He was asking some strange questions. And he said not to tell you that he and I spoke. You know I'd never keep you out of the loop bro. Give me a shout. Or let's meet up in person." What. The. Fuck. "Third message."

"Detective! I am still waiting…" Delete. Not today, Facebook Lady.

I open my desk drawer. The bottom one. I move a few case files and a legal handbook out of the way. I eye the bottle. Close bottom drawer, open top drawer. I eye a different bottle. I grab it and press the top down as I turn. Motrin. The big 800mg pills that I get from the VA. Two spill into my hand and I throw them into my mouth, washing them down with coffee. Something tells me this headache is not going away.

CHAPTER 42

I just stare and shake my head. She walks over. He raises the index finger of his left hand to her without looking up. She shakes her head. She looks at me and raises her eyebrows. I nod my head. She smiles and walks away.

"What, you gonna order without me dickhead?" Perry says, still not looking up from the menu.

"Yes, and I would be happy to order your salad and slices of pizza too."

"I think I might do something different today. Maybe the Salsiccia. What do you think?"

Alexia returns with my small Caesar salad. She looks at Perry and he smiles and nods. She shakes her head and walks away. I just stare at Perry.

"What?" he says. "So, you were right. Maybe I'll try the Salsiccia tomorrow."

"There is no tomorrow. Tomorrow is Saturday."

"Yeah, and? Karen and I might be meeting here for dinner tomorrow night. I can get it then. The Salsiccia I mean." Perry gives me a wink.

"You come here on your days off?"

"Why not? The food is good and the price is right?" He winks again.

"Please stop doing that. And you getting free food here on your days off is tacky bro. You don't think Karen notices that?"

"I'm sure she does. I suppose I could take to some high dollar restaurant like Buffoon or wherever it is that you go and spend half your paycheck. Doesn't seem worth the money to me cause I am still getting my after-dinner dessert." Another wink.

"You talk to Richie?" Perry says as Alexia drops a small salad in front of him. It's apparent that she already had it made in anticipation of his order. He doesn't seem to notice.

"What do you mean?" I push a crouton around my plate in a flanking maneuver.

"What do you mean, what do I mean? I mean, did you talk to Richie? He seems to be going pretty hard in the paint with that dead neighbor of yours."

"I haven't seen him today."

"I know. He's down at the Sheriff's Office crime lab."

I maneuver two more croutons. "Why?"

"Doing some high-speed testing on stuff he found at that dude's house. He thinks he can get some quick results. I told him not to break his neck over this. Send the routine request as usual and he will get a hit in a month. You know how he is though. A dog on a scent."

Indeed. I change the subject as best as I can. "Where are you watching the game this weekend?"

"The Fins? Don't know yet. They got a good streak going. Pulled it out against the 49ers last week for six in a row. They got the Ravens in Baltimore this week. That won't be easy. They'll shit the bed if they make the playoffs like they always do." Perry looks at my plate. "You gonna eat or just fortify your croutons against the lettuce?" Two rows of five, perfectly aligned on the right side of the plate. I'm not sure why.

"Anyway, that Army buddy of yours know your neighbor killed his kid yet?"

"He's a Marine. And it's his nephew. Baltimore huh? That'll be tough for Miami in the cold."

"Yeah, they suck in cold weather. I think they have a retractable roof on that stadium though. Maybe not. I can't remember. Anyway, you gonna tell your boy about what Richie found?"

Fuck. For the first time since I've known him, he's actually interested in a case. He's never even interested in his own.

"I don't fucking know bro. Why the fuck does it matter? Why the fuck do you care? Who gives a fucking shit what Richie finds?" I hear the increasing volume with each word I speak. I am suddenly very aware that I have Perry's full and undivided attention. I hear the beat of my heart.

"Calm down, psycho boy. I'm just asking. Richie is going to get into those buckets today or tomorrow. He's probably going to solve your missing person case for you."

Wonderful. I'll be sure to write him up for a letter of commendation for his efforts.

"Tomorrow? Tomorrow is Saturday."

"Jesus H. Are you planning on handing me a calendar next? We've already established that tomorrow is Saturday. Sarge gave Richie the green light for overtime to work this case all weekend. I told him to hit me up if he needed help this weekend. Not today of course but this weekend, reference the OT money."

Alexia drops our entrees at the table and asks if we need anything. A time machine would be nice. Maybe a one-way ticket to Mali or any other country that doesn't extradite to the United States. I just smile at her and say no.

"Perry?" He doesn't look up. I say his name again. I think I have his attention but he still doesn't look up from his food. "I have a question. Hypothetical of course. Random question."

"Send it." he says without looking up.

"If you had to do something fucked up. Like you knew it was fucked up at the time but thought it was the right thing to do, would you do it?" I have his full attention now. "Like, something criminal but not terrible." It was and is pretty fucking terrible but this is my poor attempt to minimize. "Something that may get you fired. Or worse. Would you tell anyone about it?" I hear my tone. Unstable. My words. Unsure. I would have the same expression on my face that Perry does now.

Perry's hands are now empty and placed palms apart, fingers together, forming a point over his food. Elbows on the table. Direct eye contact.

"Hypothetically, of course, what the fuck are you saying bro?" I hear his tone. Stable. His words. Sure and direct. "Do you need a lawyer?"

"Of course not! I just… I don't know. Making conversation I suppose." Perry does not look amused or convinced. He stares.

I look at Perry and say, "So, built for comfort, huh?"

An uncontrollable smile takes over his face. "Fuck yes they are! Amazing. Wanna see a picture?" I don't but I say I do anyway. I let him control the tempo of the remainder of the conversation. His tempo includes more pics and some stories that I would normally do without.

Alexia takes the empty plates away and we each throw $5 on the table and walk out.

"You heading back to the shop?" Perry asks.

"No, I am gonna bang out for the rest of the day. Run a few errands."

"Yeah, no point in going back to the office and working a case that will probably work its way out soon enough. I'll give you a shout if Richie solves it for ya." Perry says walking towards his unmarked grey 2014 Dodge Avenger.

I try to say something resembling a thank you. I try for a quip that shows me as loose and relaxed. I try for anything that may mask my true emotion. I say, "Nice car."

As Perry's face falls behind the frame of his opened door, I see his brow furrowed and his head shake from side to side. Fuck. I should be better at this.

CHAPTER 43

The drive to the home is always bittersweet. It brings me through the old neighborhood. There are a lot of great memories here. I grew up here. I drive past the park where I first played little league baseball. It doesn't look like they've done any maintenance or landscaping to that park since I played there. If I squint and use my imagination, I think I can actually see some clay underneath all of the weeds and trash littering the infield. Damn shame. This used to be a nice neighborhood. Now it is nothing less than a shithole. The home is in this neighborhood.

I thought it had only been a few months but Nicole reminded me that it had been damned near a year since I last saw him. "You should go see him," she said. "It's been too long." I assured her that it hadn't been long. She was right; it had been almost a year. This neighborhood is bittersweet. Seeing him is bittersweet.

"May I help you?"

I take in the surroundings a little before I acknowledge her greeting. These places always have a smell to them. Nothing nauseating. Just a distinct scent. This place has the aroma consistent with a thrift store, probably because most of the items here have been donated. Either that or picked up from someone's curb. I guess it's the best you can expect when a monthly social security check is footing the bill.

"Hi. I'm here to visit a resident." I say to the lady behind the counter. Roz, according to her nametag. Maybe short for Rosalyn, Rosamund, or whatever.

"And who are you visiting?" says Roz Whatever.

"William. He's in room 5 on the second floor."

"Oh Billy, we love him!" she says. Roz, short for who knows and who cares. Billy? Jesus H., he's not five years old for Christ's sake. He's a man in his sixties with probably not much time to live and he's being called Billy.

"But he's not upstairs anymore. He's a fall risk so he's on the first floor across from the nurse's station," Roz says to me. Fall risk? Damn. That doesn't have a nice ring to it.

"Are you on the list?" The voice was far away. Fall risk? His mind may be failing but he's always been so fit. How can he be a fall risk? He looked good last time I was here. A year is a long time I suppose.

"Sir!" She is staring at me. "Are you on the list?" Roz does not look amused.

"Yes. I'm his son. I'm on the list." I say as I look down at her nametag.

"It's short for Rosalina." She says smiling proudly. Who the fuck cares.

"Your father is in that room," she says gesturing across the hall. "I have some paperwork for you to sign."

I'm nearly breaking the threshold of the door as she makes the paperwork statement. I mutter something about "not signing shit" under my breath but likely loud enough for her to hear. These jackals are always trying to get you to sign something to get you on the hook for some expenses.

I stop halfway into the room and look at him. Not a sight that warms the heart. There lies a man who always had the physical strength of a lion but the inner will of a lamb. Poor life decisions have led him to this bed where now his current strength matches his prior will. Mom was the only thing that kept him balanced. When she went, so did he.

I hear it before I see it. He's watching *The Andy Griffith Show*. We used to watch that together when I was little. I haven't seen it in years. I walk over to the bed.

"Hey, Dad." The turn of his head toward me is slow. When his eyes land on mine, he looks genuinely happy.

"Hey Dad, long time. How ya been?" I say. He looks weak. He has a bandage on his forehead. Fall risk.

"Hey. I'm good," he says. The look of happiness is washed away by confusion.

"Do you remember me, Dad?" The pause answers my question long before he does.

"Remember you? Of course, I remember you, Joseph." Dad says proudly. "How could I forget you?"

With advanced stages of dementia, I've found it's best to not correct the person unless you absolutely have to. If you point out things they're saying as wrong, they can get angry, cry, or any and every emotion in between. I can try to jog his memory and risk a flood of emotions or I can spend some time with him thinking I am his youngest brother.

"How they treating ya here?"

"Oh, you know. Ok, I guess."

And so, the conversation goes for the next hour. He talks about surfing with me as kids and riding dirt bikes. The difference between the stories is the timeline. He and Uncle Joey rode Dewey Weber longboards and Bultacos. I surfed a Quiet Flight shortboard and rode a YZ80. He pushed me into waves and rode behind me on an old Honda Big Red. Same story, only a few decades later.

"Remember when I caught you smoking grass under the Lake Worth Pier with that girl?" Dad says laughing. "She was a hot little number. You thought you were in so much trouble. I still can't believe that you thought I would tell on you to mom and dad." I just sit and listen. "You should give me more credit than that. Dad would've kicked your little ass. He did mine when he caught me smoking grass. Kinda wish he kicked it a little harder. Mighta straightened me out a little." Sit. Listen. "Anyways, those were the good ole days. Right, Joey?" Right, Dad.

"Do you even remember that girl's name, Joe?"

"Her name was Rosalina." Thanks, Roz.

He laughs. "Yep, that was it. Pretty name for a pretty girl."

A few minutes pass. Maybe ten. He just watches Otis Campbell let himself out of the cell. He snickers and says something about wishing he could do that. More minutes pass. Andy teaches Opie some life lesson. Dad turns towards me. In an instant, I'm looking at a man I immediately recognize from twenty years ago. Clear blue eyes. Sharp.

"How are you doing, Son?"

It takes all of my power to maintain my composure.

"Not so good, Dad." I manage to say without my voice cracking.

"You can tell your old man anything. What's going on?" He says. His face is genuine. Focused. The confusion is gone. He appears completely aware of his surroundings.

I look at him. I feel like a little boy again. I'm staring at the strong man who would grab me by the shoulders before I went to school in the morning. His face in my face. Those blue eyes staring at me. The man who would tell me to have a good day at school, learn everything I can, and punch any bully before they punch me first. Dad hated bullies. Part of the reason I joined the military and became a cop, I think. My father of the morning was a different man from my father of the evening. Morning father was strong, determined, unstoppable. Fucking fierce. My evening father had succumbed to his vices of the day and was often barely coherent. I'm looking at my morning father.

"Dad?" I say. I guess I'm waiting for some type of permission to speak. I'm six years old again. The look he provides me gives me permission to do so.

"I killed a kid recently, Dad". I look over my shoulder to make sure that Roz is not within earshot. The doorway is clear. I am tempted to close it but I may not return to morning dad if I do. I look at him. Fierce blue eyes. He just looks at me and slightly nods.

179

"Shot him in my driveway." I stare. He nods. He would do this when I was a kid. His silence caused me to talk more and more. I do the same thing now during interrogations. Voice vacuum. Nobody likes silence.

"I shot him and dragged him to the side of my house."

"Jesus Christ, that's not good. Then what?"

"My neighbor helped me hide the body," I say and he stares. Seconds pass.

"That's a good fucking neighbor," he says. No shit, I think.

"I can't fucking sleep dad. I'm drinking more than I usually do. I'm aggro with my wife. I know the shoot was good but what I did after. I don't know why I did it. I was scared." I stop there and look over my shoulder again at the doorway.

"Nicole," He says.

"What?" Now I am the one genuinely confused.

"Your wife's name is Nicole. She's a pretty girl. Is she a good wife?" Those blue eyes.

"She's better than I deserve."

"I highly doubt that. You're a good kid. You always have been. You're the man I wish I could have been for you. Whatever you did, you had your reasons. Don't be hard on yourself. Things happen in life. Good things. Bad things. Fucking terrible things. You have to protect yourself. Protect your wife. Nobody else will. I always told you that. The only person who will take care of you is you. As much as I wanted to, I couldn't. Wouldn't. What-fucking-ever. It's done now. I'm sorry. Sorry for everything. There's no point dwelling on it. Just like the kid you shot. You had your reasons. Hell, maybe you didn't but it's done now. You need to keep it together. You can come clean and go to prison or take that to the grave with you. You need to protect yourself. You have to be number one. If you can protect your wife too, happy days." Unreal. Happy Days is now on TV. "Son, sometimes good men do bad things. Sounds like you're past the point of no return. Your only option now is to take it to the grave." He puts his hand atop mine. His hand used to dwarf mine. Now it's a frail old hand covered in liver spots and slightly grey but it still has the same effect.

In an instant, I am a groveling mess. Crying. Sobbing uncontrollably. I drop to my knees. I cry. I was lost in oblivion. Minutes pass. Maybe ten. I am brought back to the present as my dad gently patted my hand with his. I look up at him.

"You ever get in the pants of the little cutie from under the pier?" Dad says with a smile on his face. A smile with a slight glaze of confusion. I look up at the TV in time to see Fonzie thump the jukebox.

"Yeah Dad, sure did."

CHAPTER 44

Why I came here after the home, I do not know. My truck seemed to steer itself. The smell. Wooden. Still, cool, and slightly damp. I didn't like it then and I don't particularly care for it now. Poorly lit. Reminds me of a sex house case I worked. Small rooms with little screens playing retro pornography. A hole in the wall. The anonymity. The mouths on the other side of the wall underage. Gender unknown or uncared by the occupant of the room. They watch the video, close their eyes, and make their own assumptions of who it may be on the other side. Awful case and I'd love to forget it but fear I never will. The irony of this room is not lost on me.

"Hello, my son."

"Forgive me, Father, for I have sinned. It has been many years since my last confession." Fuck. This feels so strange.

"How many years my son?"

"I don't know Father. Maybe 20?" I know it has been more than that. I hope to minimize my lackluster Catholic behavior.

"After these many years, why have you decided to come today my son?"

"I need to talk. I have a confession. I trust that what I say doesn't leave this confessional? Privileged communication."

"The sacrament of confession. You will only be judged in the eyes of our Lord. I am merely his humble messenger."

I cannot quite place his accent. The last time I was in this church, albeit many years ago, I enjoyed the words of Father Mulcahy. Though I couldn't understand most of the words due to his thick Irish brogue, it was fun hearing him speak as I was a little boy. That and he being a big fan of M*A*S*H*, he insisted they used him for inspiration and would often slip in a reference to the show. I most remember some version of a prayer that involved a bag of peanuts.

"Father, I am not a bad person. At least I don't think I am. I just did a bad thing."

"Tell me, my son. This 'bad thing.' What is it?"

"I've spent my life, well most of it, my adult life that is trying to do the right thing. I served in the military. I was a medic."

"A very noble endeavor my son."

"I am a police officer now. A detective. I haven't always wanted to be a protector. It's not some self-fulfilling prophecy or anything. It just seems to have worked out that way. Anyway, something happened recently. It seemed unavoidable at the time. Still does a little. But if I had it to do over again. I don't know. I think I fucked up. Shit, sorry Padre, I didn't mean to curse."

"I understand my son. Tell me of this event in which you seem to harbor regret."

"I just… I don't know. I'm having a hard time." I find myself wondering what obligations the clergy have about reporting crimes. I think it is privileged communication but cannot quite remember. I should know this, although I've never had a priest as a witness. That may be my answer. "I killed someone, Father. Had to do it at the time. I would do it again. Maybe. But what I did after. Instead of calling it in, I did something else. I…"

"Go on my son. You need to rid yourself of this guilt. Go forth with your deed and lay yourself before the Lord."

This is fucking surreal. I cannot believe that I am about to do this.

"I hid the body, Father. Made it so it wouldn't be found."

"And you feel as though it was your only choice? That it would be your life or his?"

"Yes. He broke into my car. He had my gun in his hand."

"As is said in Exodus, 'If a thief is found breaking in and is struck so that he dies, there shall be no bloodguilt for him.' And are you familiar with Matthew 5:9 my son?"

Every cop knows it. Even if they don't know the source, they know the saying. Why the priest feels the need to invoke it right now is a little beyond me.

"Yes Father, I know it."

"Well, my son. You say that you are a law officer. Knowing the law, why not contact the authorities? Surely your status would have clarified any considerations of wrongdoing?"

"Are you familiar with the events of Ferguson, Padre?"

"Hmmm, yes quite. A conundrum I see. Do you accept Jesus as your Lord and Savior?"

"I do," I say it before I even think about it. It was a reactionary response. I think I do. I haven't really thought about it since I was a small kid.

"Say five Our Father's and five Hail Mary's but you will not be absolved of your sin until you confess your act to the authorities. I encourage you to add that as your penance and then you shall be absolved of your sin my son."

I don't say thank you as I leave the confessional. Besides the smell invoking old memories, I still feel as though I recognize the priest's accent. I fear that I may have had a case with him.

CHAPTER 45

"Hey. You seen him around today?" He has to ask twice as Perry is busy staring down her blouse. She is the first to respond.

"I haven't seen him yet today," Karen says. "Want me to call him?"

"No. No, thanks." Richie responds, leaning his upper torso into the office.

"We had lunch earlier. He said something about running errands." Perry gives the air quotes and his usual wink when he says 'errands.' "He's probably floating in his pool as we speak. Can't say that I blame him. It's nice outside."

"How was he?" Richie asks.

"Fine. Why?"

"No reason. See you guys later. Don't mention to him that I was looking for him, ok?" Richie says. By this time Perry has turned back around and affixed his stare back to Karen's cleavage.

"How did the crime lab do? Any hits?" Karen asks.

With only a slight profile visible to her she could hear Richie say, "Yeah. I got one." As the last word was said, he left her view.

"That was a little weird," Karen says. She is looking at Perry's eyes but her gaze is not returned.

"Probably not that weird. You know how Richie is when he's working a case. He gets way too into it." Perry looks up and into her eyes. "I don't think Richie's too far off though. He did say something strange at lunch today. I wouldn't tell Richie this but..."

"What?" asks Karen.

Perry looks at her, then at the open door to the office. He closes the door and walks back to her, looking directly into her eyes. "Listen to this."

Karen listened. She was sure to lean over her desk while Perry talked. Leaning into someone speaking is a sure sign of active listening. Leaning into someone speaking with excessive buttons of your blouse opened to reveal ample cleavage is a sure sign of active manipulation. Karen knows this. Perry, as an observer, would recognize this. As a participant, he is hypnotized by D-cup breasts and may not be in full control of his utterances. She listens and formulates her opinion. When Perry is finished staring and talking, she tells him to leave. That she has work to do. She gives him a wink and tells him that she will "see him" later.

Every police agency has an internal phone list of emergency contacts. If something terrible happens to an officer, one does not want to waste time scrambling to find the phone number for a wife or husband. It is incumbent on the agency to do a notification. Having a loved one find out from the news or social media is highly frowned upon. These lists are accessible by anyone in the agency for this purpose. They are usually used for non-emergent reasons such as getting info for a surprise party, retirement, etc. Karen pulls the list. She finds the number she was hoping for. "A glass of wine sounds great! It will be nice to catch up," the voice says on the other line.

CHAPTER 46

He was asleep when she got home. He texted her earlier and said he had a rough day. Nicole didn't ask any questions. She wanted to give him a little space. She seized the opportunity to spend a Friday evening with her sister. After all, they had a nice dinner at Buccano this week. When she got home, he was fast asleep in the guest room. She could tell that he had been drinking. There was an empty bottle of Knob Creek by the refrigerator. That's the spot recyclables go before they get put in the bin in the garage. She took the bottle and made her way to the bin, eyeing the Harley in the garage. She hoped for a breakfast ride in the morning.

Morning came. No husband and no bike. Nicole was surprised to find a note on the kitchen counter: *You were asleep. Went for ride on bike. Need a little time to chill. I'll be back later. Enjoy your day. Love you.* Disappointment set in but before it could turn to annoyance, her phone rang. Nicole did not recognize the number but answered regardless. She feared for her husband's safety when he was on the bike and risked answering a spam caller. As she said hello, the caller introduced themselves.

"We've met before but never really chatted. Is there a possibility that we can meet today? Alone." Before Nicole could formulate a response, the voice said "Let's grab coffee in an hour. That new boutique coffee shop by the beach. My treat. I have a few things to run past you. Best to keep it between us for now." All Nicole could say was "OK" before the line went dead. She found it a little puzzling, but before her puzzlement could build the doorbell rang.

Although having never met him in person, she knew immediately who it was at her door. She opened and before she could make any introduction, he said, "Is Doc here?" When she politely shook her head, Woody asked if he could come in. "Nicole, I am so sorry to bother you. I think we need to talk."

CHAPTER 47

Fear. That's the most accurate description of the look on their faces. Not only fear. There was also frustration, desperation, and confusion. Primarily just fear though. I suppose that's an understandable reaction for all of us to have. I know how this ends.

Just five minutes prior, I was fast asleep in my bed. Then, BOOM! It was a sound I know all too well. The flash sound diversionary device, commonly referred to as a 'flashbang.' It produces a thunderous sound that registers at 175 decibels. A jet engine at 100 feet is not that loud. The flashbang also emits light at over one million candela. Having one detonate near you is akin to having a lightning bolt strike at your feet. Oh yeah, it's hot too. The heat and the light didn't affect me as it went off outside of my bedroom window. It was meant to distract me. Also meant to distract me was the breaking of the glass window in the family room of my house and the breaking in, referred to as breaching, of my front door. This all happened simultaneously. SWAT teams

191

conduct these coordinated strikes to cause tactical confusion to the target. To throw off their OODA loop.

My initial reaction was to shield Nicole with my body. My instinct to protect her. With the hate and discontent which was consuming my home, all I wanted to do was protect my wife. The beautiful woman of my dreams. My world. My everything.

I hurled my body to her side of the bed and came crashing down atop her pillow. My body sprawled across her side of the bed covering the entire area where she should have been.

That was five minutes ago. That was when the amplified voice was coming across the loudspeaker. "This is the Palm Beach County Sheriff's Office SWAT team serving a search warrant." Surround and call-out procedures. "Will the occupant of 1005 Ridgewood Court please exit the residence with your hands up." It is much safer to do that than to enter a residence when you have a target with access to firearms. "We have your home surrounded. This is the Palm Beach County Sheriff's Office SWAT team serving a search warrant." I think I recognize his voice. "Will the occupant of 1005 Ridgewood Court please exit the residence with your hands up." I think that may be Axtell. We went to the academy together. He went to the Sheriff's Office and I went to the local PD.

Fear. The few eyes that I can see among the blinding spotlights and takedown lights oriented at me say it all. Fear.

Despite what the national news media may want you to believe about cops, the overwhelming majority of police never shoot anyone. Virtually none of them want to shoot anyone, especially if that someone is another police officer. Fear. Fear that they may have to shoot a cop.

Five minutes ago, I was sleeping nude in my bed. Now I am standing in my driveway. I am holding my Springfield XD-9. "Keep your finger straight and off the trigger until you are ready to fire." I can hear his voice in my head. "Doc, you get that? Don't touch that trigger until you're ready to get some." It sounds like a lifetime ago but SSgt Rodriguez's voice is still clear in my head. 'Hot Rod' some people referred to him as. He was a bad dude. He taught the marksmanship at FMSS. My finger is straight and off the trigger.

Fear. No cop wants to shoot another cop. No cop wants to believe the allegations that are probably written in the search warrant probable cause affidavit. Fear. I know how this ends.

I look over and see a LENCO BearCat. I wonder if Nicole is in there. I don't remember her getting out of bed. Actually, I don't remember her being home when I put the bike in the garage. I wonder when they got her out of the house. Did she know yesterday? Today?

She's probably not in the BearCat. They probably have her in a mobile command station a few blocks away. Maybe even back at the PD.

"Drop the gun Detective. This is not necessary. We just want to talk to you."

Naked. Except for the gun held down by my side.

Fear.

You may want to call it cop privilege. Maybe fear. But the two SWAT officers who had .300 Blackout rifles pointed through the window of my family room had every reason and opportunity to 'take the shot' as I walked out of my bedroom with a gun in my hand. Naked. Gun by my side.

Every other situation would have likely had those officers 'neutralize the threat' when presented with a man with a gun. Action is faster than reaction and they have no obligation to wait for me to shoot first. They didn't shoot me. Fear. Or cop privilege.

Standing in my driveway. Naked. Fear.

"This does not need to happen this way. We can just talk."

The SWAT surround and call-out procedures have ended. Crisis negotiations have begun. I don't see him but Richie is watching from the backseat of a patrol car.

I think about Nicole. I think about how I am standing in virtually the same spot as that young fella was when I shot him. I think about Woody.

"Detective, we want to hear your side. You have a lot to live for. We want to talk to you. Your wife wants us to tell you that she loves you." Her name is Nicole. I love her. I love her so much. I think she has always worried about the piece of me she never met.

Fear. The fear in the eyes of the officers who still have their rifles pointed at me. The fear in my eyes at the sound of an oncoming train approaching. I know how this ends. My finger is no longer straight and off the trigger. Fear.

CHAPTER 48

Richie knew the landscape well. As well as anyone could; however, this was his first time viewing from this vantage point. The sounds. The smell. He is usually seated in a different area. He rests his head in his hands, the metal pressing the area under his nose. This is a new smell for him.

"Detective Mitchell. I would like to ask you a few questions about how you came to this conclusion. First, can you please identify the defendant?"

She points to Richie but knows this is only for dramatic effect as she plays to the jury. She needs to verbalize the description for the stenographer to record. It went on for hours. She spoke about her relationship with Perry. The pillow talk they had. The leads he inadvertently provided her. She smiles as she thinks that a blow job is as effective as any truth serum.

She talks about her conversation with Tracy Richardson. How she allowed Tracy to be the amateur sleuth that she always wished she was. How Tracy solicited her information. Pillow talk once removed.

How she contacted her friend at the crime lab to find out the DNA hit information that Richie received. How he told his technician buddy to keep the information under wraps. Fellatio is a great way to solicit information.

How she went to the Inspector General to circumvent her own agency in the belief that she may be stonewalled. She talks about the probable cause that she established for the search warrant. She talks about her interview with Nicole. Her interview with Gunnery Sergeant Woodside.

Richie has his head in his hands, the chain of his handcuffs digging deeper into the flesh that lies below his blonde mustache. He recalls sitting in the back of the cruiser. He had a clear line of sight. Richie was sure that they would shoot him dead if he raised the gun. His fellow detective. He considered him a friend. He recalls the gun being raised. He recalls the firing of multiple 40-millimeter non-lethal direct impact rounds. Richie saw the impact to the chest and abdomen area. He watched as the gun fell from his hand and he fell to the ground, writhing in pain. He watched as multiple SWAT operators swarmed him, each taking a limb. Richie watched as he was secured with flex cuffs and placed into a marked police car. The same type of car that he was watching from. The back caged prisoner area. Richie had logged thousands of miles behind the wheel of a marked cruiser before becoming a detective but never one foot as a passenger in the back seat. Until that day, nearly two years ago. Now he is listening to Karen provide the full details of her investigation. An investigation that was his. Until he tried to protect a friend. He can only pray that he doesn't receive the same fate.

"Detective Mitchell. What do you feel should happen to Bradley Richardson?" The prosecutor asks.

"Well, it is my true belief that he is an accessory after the fact to second-degree murder. Due to that, he should receive the same life sentence as given to the person who committed said murder."

The prosecutor looks at the judge and says, "No further questions your Honor."

CHAPTER 49

Richie walks in. He is holding his sheets, a pillow, an extra jumpsuit, and a small toiletry bag. He can't bring himself to make eye contact with him. He just stands there. Stiff and staring. Finally, he brings himself to say, "Why did you do it?"

I anticipated the question. I had thought about the answer. I was going to tell him everything. I had planned to apologize. I sat up on my bunk to look at Richie. Our eyes meet. Richie has tears building in his. Top lip trembling. The question fills the air. It is the only thing in the room right now and there is no ignoring it.

I look Richie up and down. I have rehearsed this every day that I have been inside. I take a deep breath and look into Richie's eyes. "Nice jumpsuit," I say. I lay back down into my bunk, fold my hands behind my head, and close my eyes to rest.

ACKNOWLEDGEMENTS

First and foremost, you! Thank you very much for reading this book. If you liked it, please let me know. If you hated it, you can always use it to prop up a table, or as a door stop, or as tinder to start a fire.

My wife, who puts up with me. Thank you for the encouragement to keep writing this book. You are amazing.

LJ, for the motivation to write and for using your name (without your permission, no less).

A few select friends, who had no idea I used them as inspiration. Sorry, not sorry.

And the many authors who I looked to for inspiration and guidance. I would list you here but fear the list would be too long and you may not care to be associated with my writing. Plus, my wife has already accused me of "fangirling" over one particular writer and I do not want to push him further toward getting a restraining order than he already might be!

ABOUT THE AUTHOR

W.C. Gordon is a law enforcement officer and a military veteran. He lives at his home in South Florida with his wife and dog. The Detective Next Door is his first novel.

Instagram: @authorwcgordon
E-mail: authorwcgordon@gmail.com

CPSIA information can be obtained
at www.ICGtesting.com
Printed in the USA
LVHW051802151120
671757LV00013B/1700

9 780578 680064